From Pulpit to Purgatory

ELOISE C. JACOBS-BRUNNER

TO MY FAMILY

1

The dead woman's father and mother stood by the window of the church house staring into the evening's gloom. Her younger brother and sister, feeling restless from the day-long mourning left the gloomy verandah and trudged the woodlands of the churchyard to relieve their heartache. Those woods, over which freed blacks travelled a century earlier to join the Revolutionary War, were now wetted with the salty tears of worn and weary runaway slaves escaping their masters in the South. All of those tears of misery now mingled with the tears of the mourners gathered around the old verandah of the church house that evening.

The dead woman's mother and father glanced down the length of the verandah every now and then in the direction of Reverend Jeffrey, husband of their dead daughter. Reverend Jeffrey stood alone in a small corner of the vast decaying verandah, his lean young body hunched over in dejection. Those looking towards the end of the verandah saw nothing but a blurry mass amidst the dancing shadows from the live oaks hanging over the portico. To the Olivetti Church-going villagers, Reverend Jeffrey was a man of good character, solemn and placid with a ready remedy for lost souls. Everyone said he was humble in all he said and all he did, and the only time he ever allowed himself to brag, was to tell that he never yawned in church when he was a young boy. Unlike other boys his age, he never yawned once, because he loved to listen to the minister's word, and he knew without a single doubt that one day, he too, would stand upon a pulpit and bring sinners into his fold.

Now here he was, weak with distress, hanging onto the verandah railings and wondering how did this calamity come to have fallen upon his head, and how will he be able to tell his congregation that he did not murder his wife, Sarah. His head hung low and touched the railings as if looking for an answer. The old verandah where they were all gathered, with its old shakes and beams seemingly as worn and as exhausted as the mourners themselves, squeaked and groaned in response. So intent was young minister Jeffrey on his own sorrow that he could not respond to the gloomy hellos that passed his ears, or the sympathetic pat on the shoulder that came and went over the last few hours.

The frightened friends, villagers, and church members who had earlier passed through the iron gates and into the church house all day long, gathered in little knots on the vast wooden verandah to discuss and contemplate their sorrows. Putting their heads together in private conversation, they wailed and whispered about the bad-luck that had descended upon the dear young minister and his family since he took over control of the parish only one year earlier.

"That was a most powerful death. I still......." And the frightened whisper trailed off into the dark.

"No sense in it at all. Who knew, two deaths in the space of one year, and no one knows why," whispered Mrs. Bailey, the church soprano. "Until now, I was never afraid of death, but now, I just don't know."

" And how can a little, little town like ours, so little, you need a dozen lanterns to find it in broad daylight, how can a little place such as this have two untimely deaths in one family in the space a few months?" asked a meek-looking man in the group.

"And from the same church house too. If only someone could answer that," replied Mr. Phillip, the shopkeeper, shaking his head from side to side.

As the evening deepened, a hushed silence lay uneasily over the mourners, and all questions seeking answers ceased. One of the mourners, Mr. Jebdiah Bennet, whose job it was to polish and shine the church benches every Saturday evening, and light the vestry candles every Sunday mornings, stepped away from the group and entered the kitchen. He lit two lamps and three lanterns and put them in various parts of the verandah to brighten the house. Then he lit the kitchen stove, and from the enormous chimney smoke billowed, and the smell of burning wood filled the air.

"That's a mighty good smell. It will take my mind off this calamity for a little while," said one.

"Yes, Yes," they all agreed.

With most of the villagers visiting the house of the dead, the little houses along the village streets with their gabled roofs and Dutch windows were dark. A few mourners noticed for the first time that their houses look like large stumps outlined against the evening sky. No lights shone from the windows. Except for the houses with the infirmed or the sick, no evening lamps shone along the village streets. Dinner time had come and gone, but still no one moved from the church house porch to go home and light their evening fires.

"Never before seen my house from afar. Just look! In the near dark, it's as if we're looking at a large graveyard."

"No, no, stop that kind of talk. Your frightened mind is playing tricks on you. Everything looks ghostlike in the dark," said a voice of reason.

"It reminds me I need to go home and cook dinner, but God knows, my stomach is full, so full of grief," said another.

Just as Reverend Jeffrey was contemplating the dark streets from the vast verandah, he heard a rough clearing of a throat and he turned his head to see two Elders of the Olivetti Church, Mr. Morrison and Mr. Harrison, their faces grave, but dignified shuffling their worn bodies towards the young minister.

"Jeffrey, my boy, how did things come to this?" the First Elder asked, clearing his throat again with much energy.

The energetic old voice woke the young minister from his discomfort and he answered.

"I don't know how things have come to this. Things were normal, very normal for the last few weeks and if the good Lord..." and his thoughts strayed, and his voice trailed off and the young minister fell silent. A full minute passed before he spoke again.

"You know, when the thunder rolls, and the lightning makes that grand fork in the sky and my Sarah is gone, I wonder if ...."

"Wonder if what?" whispered the second Elder, moving his face as close as he could to the young Reverend.

"I wonder if I'm a man fit to preach God's word and His wonders."

"What do you mean, my boy," asked the second Elder in confusion. When the young minister remained silent, the Elder continued.

"Jeffrey, you are a confused man at the moment, so this is my advice to you. You must avoid and prevent rumors of any kind. Sarah was your wife, so watch what you do, and watch what you say, because you will be criticized, and scrutinized and moralized by the very people who look up to you."

Jeffrey's frightened naked eyes shone through the dark as he listened to the Elder's advice. Feeling them closing in on him, and their piercing eyes judging him, Reverend Jeffrey took two steps backwards from the Elders as they spoke.

"But now you need rest and some peace. In the meantime, show your sorrow and grief for a full year. A full year without any joy, my boy. Wear sackcloth and walk in ashes, and pray in ashes if you must, my child. But show that outward sorrow for a full year. That will be your only peace and rest. Now some quiet and good sleep will do you some good. May God go with you."

As the three stood silent, the sun sank behind the low mountains and disappeared. Darkness fell, and as though it were the signal the mourners were waiting for, a single note pierced the evening air and Mr. Phillip's bass came through loud and clear. The women joined in and then the men, and soon the old verandah was rocking and sway-ing with the sorrowful weight of the many mourners pouring out a dirge for the departed Sarah. The singing went on for several minutes and then it became quieter and quieter until the only voice left was Mr. Phillip's, whose octave reached over the treetops and down to the graveyard where Sarah's sister and brother stood listening. The two stood amongst the autumn leaves, amongst the stillness of the grave-stones, where their sister's body would be laid to rest later that week. They felt the stillness of the place. No crickets, or katydids or the sounds of the frogs in the nearby pond came through. "It's as though the whole place is in mourning," her sister whispered, as they gazed into the dark and listened.

Feeling cleansed and relieved of sorrow's weight, the mourners left the church house and went home. The house became quiet, unusually quiet. Leaving the decaying verandah, Reverend Jeffrey strolled quietly through the house closing doors and windows. The house suddenly seemed small and mean and he felt it closing in on him. The calmness and the seren-ity it once held for him were now gone. On his way to the bedroom, he paused to listen. The night noises were gone. Even the usual brays and neighs from the horse barn were gone. "So very quiet," he whispered to the dark. Reverend Jeffrey blew out the lamp, crawled into bed and pulled the bedcovers high over his head.

One week later, the autopsy was completed. That afternoon, the villag-ers stepped out in their Sunday finery to bury Sarah. A procession Sarah would have been proud of turned their heads towards the church cem-etery. To show their deep sorrow for the dead, the mourners left behind, in the town square, carriages, horses, buggies, and mules and marched with weary legs to the cemetery. The men scrubbed clean, shaved and dressed in shirts that had been boiled for hours, and the women dressed in black with purple streamers that frightened the birds, marched from the village square to the churchyard, two miles away. Street sweepers in their grey uniforms splattered with blobs of mud, and chimney sweepers covered in soot, all stopped their daily chores as the procession passed by. Once in a while, one or two women fainted away and relatives or friends had to search her bosom for the tell-tale handkerchief filled with tiny crystals of smelling salts. Finding it, they held it close to her nose until her eyes flut-tered and she came to.

As they marched, the bells of the little church began its toll for the dead. A quiet hush fell over the marchers, and quivering lips became silent. As they listened to the mournful toll, they clasped their hands up to Heaven and prayed for the soul of Sarah.

After the funeral, rumors took over the lives of the little village. They wondered silently, they wondered loudly if their dearly beloved, young minister was to be blamed for his wife's death. The rumors pitted wives and husbands against each other, friends against friends, one side feeling that there was no way under God's green earth that the young minster would have done such an awful thing, and the other side knowing, without a doubt, that he had done it. The discussions broke the monotony of people's dull lives, and interspersed the sultry autumn days with vim and verve. Corn and wheat harvesting were hurried, wash left undone, and sewing and knitting left for another day. Market baskets filled with meat, eggs, and fish sat on doorsteps while neighbors, friends and enemies leaned against garden gates and dissected and examined the little lives of Reverend Jeffrey and his family.

"The dear wife gone, the sister gone, only dear God knows why?" worried voices sounded off.

"Notice how he didn't join us when we gathered at the church house to mourn with him, never once, but stood by himself in a corner of the verandah all evening long?"

"Yes, yes, didn't even thank us for coming to mourn with him," another pointed out.

"Quite right, after I hurried up that morning to cook, and clean, and sew, and make apple dumplings so I could get to the church house in time. It was as if he didn't even know I was there mourning with him."

"Oh, the poor Reverend was in distress," piped in a voice of reason. "Don't go thinking he didn't see you. I bet he knew every name who was there mourning with him that evening. Remember, his poor wife had just died suddenly. Poor thing, in such distress and wondering all sorts of- God knows what."

"Two weeks now, and rumors and whispers saying the very same thing," said another.

"A thousand shame on you people for listening to such ugliness," Mr. Jeb Bennet admonished them. "He be our minister and savior, and a good one he is too. That poor man should have been born a saint."

The whispers and rumors reached the ear of the Reverend three weeks after the funeral. As he left the barn one morning where he just hidden a group of runaway slaves and was walking up to the back door of the church house, he heard the clip clop of horses' hoofs approaching. He glanced towards the barn door and then at the horse and buggy galloping towards the house. As it came through the gate, Reverend Jeffrey sighed gratefully. It was Philip, the shopkeeper who knew all of his secrets. No one but Phillip knew the Reverend's big secret: that he stowed runaway slaves in his barn, sometimes outback underneath bales of straw or logs of wood, or even up in tall trees where the dense leaves hid them from sight. Phillip jumped down from the buggy, lifted two bags of horse feed from the back and deposited them on the back porch. Then he came and stood beside the Reverend and whispered:

"Reverend, I come earlier than usual because I want you to know a few things. Not a single word came out of me. You must know that. Nobody knows about that rat poison, and nobody can guess it either."

The Reverend became confused, his eyes suddenly going blank and he looked at Phillip with much sorrow, as though Phillip himself had gone mad. "I'm not following you Phillip. What are you talking about?"

And amidst the twittering birds, and the horses and carriages galloping up and down the village street, the Reverend heard Philip say. "It's all over town, Reverend. Every time I turn around, I hear somebody wondering if you did it to your poor wife."

A little cry escaped the Reverend lips and he covered his face with his hands as if to hide the shame that had befallen him. Then he fell heavily into one of the porch chairs and put his hands over his heart. His lungs felt as if they had collapsed; he could not breathe. "Dear God, Oh God, my life is over. Dear God," he said in a faint voice.

Phillip came closer and bent over the Reverend's chair. "No, no Reverend. You must not say that. I know you did nothing to your dear wife. No, your life isn't over."

"So, why the rumors and gossips?"

"Because you are a good man and people naturally just wondering if their good Reverend would do such a thing." Philip looked away as he said this, his face full of pain. "There is another reason I'm come, Reverend."

"Another reason. What do you mean?"

"To help you get away until this thing blow over." You must run away from here. I don't want to hear any more gossips and rumors. You've got to go away."

Reverend Jeffrey shook his head in disbelief. "No, No. I won't run away. I've done nothing wrong. God knows I have no reason to hide from His face."

"But Reverend...." and Phillip's voice trailed off as footsteps came up the walkway and an urgent knock came to front door.

The Reverend beckoned to Phillip to stay quiet while he stood up and went to answer the knock. At the doorway he came face to face with two stern-looking men dressed as police detectives.

"Are you Reverend Jeffrey Masters?" one asked roughly.

Taken back by the gruff greeting at the door, the Reverend did not answer right away. So the gruff voice continued.

"Your wife's family has brought charges against you," he said, handing the Reverend an official looking document.

"Reverend Jeffrey hesitated. Then he opened his lips to protest, but nothing came out. Finally he said, "As God is my witness, I did not harm my wife. I'm a man of God. I am a Reverend. I look after my flock." Then he continued his voice shaking and trembling. "I would never think of harming not even the least of them and..."

Before he could complete his sentence, the first detective interrupted, " Reverend, the law will decide that. We will be back after the autopsy results come in so please, do not leave town."

With that final warning, the two men turned and left the trembling Reverend staring after them. Then he heard Philip's voice trying to comfort him. "Heard every word they said, Reverend, and it seems to me you be in dire trouble. They are coming to get you. You gotta run away now Reverend, not tomorrow, or the next day, but now. I will help you."

A quiet sob left the Reverend's trembling lips. "I don't know. I have done nothing wrong. The Good Lord knows that. I won't run."

"All right Reverend, I am leaving now, but I'll be here anytime you need my help."

After the shopkeeper left, the Reverend stood rooted to the spot, his head hung in deep thought. Several minutes later, whispering voices reached him and he turned around to see the group of runaway slaves whispering amongst themselves. They moved closer to him.

"Good Reverend," the leader of the group said, "we look out through the crack in the side of the barn and we see and hear everything the two lawmen said. Good Reverend, God know you did no such a thing, but Reverend, you gotta leave this place. You must run fast from this place, Good Reverend," he said, choking with emotion.

The Reverend became visibly irritated, his jaw tightening with rage. "No, No, I won't run. The detectives will be back and they will see I have nothing to hide. No I won't run away," he said firmly.

But the head of the runaway slaves was not ready to give up on the good Reverend.

"Good Reverend, look at me, my wife here and three children, and all these other negro slaves. We done nothing wrong, but if the law find us, they will make sure we be guilty of something. Yes, they will send us back down the river." Without skipping a beat, he continued, "Good Reverend, we know a place where you can run and bide your time till better days come."

The Reverend remained silent, his eyes turned towards Heaven. The group of slaves stood and waited. After what seemed like an eternity, they heard him say.

"What place is this?"

"This is it Reverend. A place in Virginny. They will hide you till such time."

"Virginny?"

"Yes, they took my wife and me and the little 'uns when we find ourselves running from the whip, the dogs, the heat, the hunger."

"Oh you mean Virginia?"

"About half a day's ride from Cabbage Hill. A big grey house with a high wood fence around it. You can't miss it Reverend. Just use the usual code."

"Yes, the code!"

"Remember, don't go to the front door and knock. They won't answer any knock. You must go to the window and scratch, or whistle. When they answer, you just say, "Mount Gilead" or "William Penn.""

"Oh that I know. I've been hiding runaways for years now," the Reverend reminded them.

"We move on tonight, Reverend. Going to follow the Northstar up to Canada before the cold weather come upon us. So God go with you, Good Reverend."

2

Later that evening, Reverend Jeffery stood at the iron gate of the church house awaiting his future. He stood, shifting his weight from one foot to the other, staring down the road leading to town and wondering what he should do next. Would the Good Lord please give him a sign, he prayed. People rushing home from town hailed him. Evening lamps went on one by one in houses along the road, then they went out one by one, but still the Reverend stood by the gate. The full moon rose over the big barn, yet the Reverend stood rooted by the iron gate. When the church bell rang out the midnight hour, he merely pulled out his pocket watch to check the time.

Four hours later when the church bell announced the hour, the Reverend was ready to move. He stepped with bold strides away from the gate and marched into the house like someone who had just received a long-awaited answer. He marched through the front parlor, then the inner parlor, and for the next half hour he opened and closed drawers as though searching for something. Then for a moment he stood still. Then he rushed to open a small door underneath the window. He pulled out a box, rummaged through layers of papers and documents and found a bag of coins. Afterwards, he raced into the kitchen where he grabbed several large empty bags which Philip, the shopkeeper, used to bag flour and corn. They were folded neatly on the shelves to be used as clothing for runaways. He pulled out a drawer and took out a large shearing scissors.

Taking the shears he snipped off enough fabric to make three holes large enough to fit over a man's head and arms. He slipped it on and it fell over his body like a long gown worn by the prophets of old. Taking a piece of rope, he tied it at the waist. Afterwards he grabbed from his desk his old worn Bible, a satchel, some matches, a knife, then his coat and hat and headed out of the house.

In a few minutes his buggy was clip clopping down the road towards the center of town. He slowly passed through the village, passed the mill, the general store, and the night patrollers' house. Young boys pushing wheelbarrows with newspapers called out the latest news.

"Arsenic found in stomach. Read all about it. Arsenic Found in Stomach of Reverend's Wife."

A few early risers, farmers and street cleaners on their way to work hailed the Reverend. Some whispered, others stopped and stared at the Reverend wearing sack cloth like the prophets in the Bible, and riding unhurriedly through town.

"He must be going to visit to the sick now and lick a few sinners later."

"But you know they are coming soon to carry him off to jail."

"Yes, siree, only a matter of time now."

Pretending not to hear the call of the newsboys, or the gossip of the people, the Reverend rode slowly along. The villagers did not drop their gaze. They held it until the Reverend and his buggy were out of sight. As soon as he turned the corner and was no longer visible, the Reverend smiled a bitter smile; he was glad he had decided to leave town. It was only a matter of time before the law came to get him. He soon rounded another bend, briefly looked backwards and then pulled on the reins. The buggy sped to a gallop and did not stop until one hour later when it reached the railroad station of New Rivertown. Coach 1656 to Cabbage Hill was waiting in the station. At the station, Reverend Jeffrey looked around. Ten minutes before departure. He sat in his buggy wondering what to do with those ten minutes. And what to with the horse and buggy. Should he sell them? No. No time to bargain and haggle, he thought. He grabbed a piece of paper from amongst his package, and wrote "Free Horse & Buggy" in bold letters. Then he jumped off, bought his ticket and got on the train with eight other passengers. He sat by himself in the back coach.

At noon the following day, Reverend Jeffrey arrived in Cabbage Hill, Virginia. It was a crowded station, and he sat on the train until the crowd had thinned out. Then he stepped out and looked around. A buggy with driver was what he needed. He saw a sign pointing to "livery stable." He hurried down the lane. At the livery stable he paid for a buggy and driver. As he was about to leave, he spied a wanted poster nailed to a wall near the doorway. He moved closer to take a look, and there he came face to face with a drawing of his own face staring back at him. He turned away in disbelief. His legs shook under him. He turned to look at the poster again. It read: 'WANTED MAN: Reward: $500 for His Capture.' The Reverend studied the drawing of the wanted man. Yes, that was him, same square face, but those features? Those hardened eyes and mouth. Had his face become so hard and mean over the past year? The Reverend knew he had to move on, so he pulled his hat low on his forehead to hide his face and was soon on his way.

Sometime past midnight, the Reverend's buggy reached the big grey house with the high wooden fence. They rode through an open gate and down a long path to the front door of the house where two lighted lanterns hung. The Reverend got down from the buggy and the driver turned around, rode through the gate and disappeared into the night.

When buggy and driver were out of sight, Reverend Jeffrey moved to the side of the house and scratched three times on a window. A voice from inside answered.

"Who might you be?"

"From Mount Gilead," the Reverend answered.

The door opened slowly and cautiously and Reverend Jeffrey showed his face. Then the door opened wider and the Reverend entered. A figure wearing a religious garb bore down on him.

"I can tell you aren't one of our usual persecuted people. Who are you?" the figure asked.

"An innocent man persecuted by the laws of man."

"Heavens forbid, what do you mean?"

The law says I have killed my wife, but I am innocent. I am a minister of God. I save souls, not destroy them."

The figure studied the Reverend's face for a few seconds and then invited him to sit at the table. When they were seated, the figure asked again. "Why would anyone say you've killed your wife?"

"I don't know. I just don't know." The Reverend rested his chin in his hand, tapped his fingers on the table, and searched his memory for every little detail he could use to convince the figure in the dark that he was indeed a persecuted soul. "It's a long story," the Reverend answered, "but if you have the time, I will tell it."

"Yes, do tell your story. It is dark, it is late and we do have the time. Please tell us your story," he insisted.

The Reverend needed no time to think. As soon as the elder Quaker had stopped speaking, the Reverend began. "You see, it all started when I turned eighteen years old; I knew, even before then that my calling was to serve God. I have always known it since I had sense enough to know. Could always feel it in my bones, so my parents sent me to study the ministry. I took my Ordination Vows at age twenty-six. I remember the Bishop's hand resting on my head. It was strong, and warm, and holy. And when he asked if I would diligently devote my life to the church, and to make myself an efficient minster of Jesus Christ, I answered, "I will do so with the Lord being my Helper."

The Reverend paused to relive the moment, then he continued. His first real service, he said, was one month later. It was a beautiful service, with people from all over Bellville, the aged, the young, the infirmed, all kinds came to worship at his church: The Olivetti Church of God. He remembered the road leading to the church was full of wagons, buggies, mules, and donkeys kicking up dust ten feet high as they hurried to the church yard. People pitched tents and stayed all day. Then one Sunday, a few weeks later, an especially large crowd came because it was picnic day, the last Sunday in October. He mingled with the crowd, he said, getting to know the many names and faces. As he stood speaking to a small knot of his congregants, he said, he heard a demanding voice behind him.

He turned around to see a big woman; she stood high above him, about age thirty, with shiny spectacles falling off her nose. There she was barking orders to her slave and afterwards she made tracks towards him.

"Oh Reverend," she said, "remember me, Mrs. Jeremiah. Been meaning to speak to you. Such a glorious service this morning. But first, I want to introduce you to my sister, Sarah."

And she rolled on without giving him a chance to speak.

" Sarah works at the mill in town. Does spinning, and carding and all manner of things at the factory. Does a nice job on her own dresses too. But all the same I'm just full of thanksgiving that she does work and bring home money to give old ma and pa."

Before the Reverend could answer, other people came up to try to speak with him.

"Reverend, tis a blessing having you amongst us today. We men mighty pleased because we know you will bring harmony between all the waring families in this village."

"Waring families, how so?"

"Oh, yes, waring families been fighting each other for generations now. Real bad feelings between families. Fighting over everything and nothing."

"Then, I do hope I will be able to bring harmony to this village," the Reverend told them.

The following Sunday Mrs. Jeremiah approached him again after church services. She scolded him for ditching her in the middle of their conversation last Sunday. When he did not reply, because he couldn't remember who she was, she went on.

"My sister, Sarah, remembers you from her school days. Do you remember her, Reverend?"

"No, no, I'm sorry, I don't recollect."

"That is quite all right Reverend; we can remedy that. I am inviting you and my Sarah to dinner next Sunday."

"We will see, Mrs. Jeremiah, we will see," the Reverend said. "Now please excuse me while I go over and greet the group standing over there," he said pointing to a knot of women.

The Reverend left and moved amongst other groups, learning the names and faces of those who had come to hear his sermon.

Later that afternoon, in the living room of the church house, sometimes called the inner parlor, the Reverend was sitting at his shabby desk with its ink-stained runner lit by two candles at each end. Two threadbare chairs and an old sofa curved near a wall. On his desk sat a goose-feathered pen and a bottle of ink. A cat-o-nine for whipping sinners hung on the opposite wall. The Reverend had just rummaged through a pile of old linen rags and had cut each into precise rectangular pieces all of the same size. He picked up a few pieces of rags, dipped his pen into ink and began to write.

Every few minutes, an old slave woman popped her head into the doorway. She stood silently by the door, shook her head wearily several times, and then retreated behind the door. Once in a while she came directly into the living room and laid before the Reverend extra pieces of linen which he added to the pile. Each time the old woman entered the room, the minister ignored her and continued to dip his pen and ink and write something on the pieces of cloth. Every now and then the Reverend held up a piece of linen to the light and read the big words that filled the length of each piece of cloth:

> "If my people shall humble themselves, and pray and seek
> my face, and turn from their wicked ways, then Heaven
> will forgive them their sins and heal their land."

> 11 Chronicle Ch. 7:14

After reading his handiwork, his face beamed with pride and a low satisfied gurgle escaped his throat. He continued to work late into the evening, stopping now and then to count the growing pile of linen, while ignoring the old woman who kept popping in and out of the room.

Finally, he set his pen down and counted the linens: one hundred and seventy sheets, one for each church family.

"Yes, one for each family. This should get them talking to each other, and working together to heal their land," he said out loud to no one, "and soon enemies will become friends. Ah yes." And the Reverend leaned back into his chair, folded his arms and closed his eyes.

Half an hour later, the old slave woman popped her head through the doorway and seeing that the Reverend had completed his work, she watched him rest, like a small satisfied child with no care upon his head. As she watched him sleep, she tried to remember the hundreds of little things he would tell her about his work. These things she dutifully filed away in her head and kept them there like a sealed vault holding precious goods. She shared these precious goods with no one but the Reverend, and every evening before he went to bed, she would called out to him and remind him who or what needed his help the following day or the following week. Now as she stood before him with his eyes closed, she called out to him.

"Mr. Reverend, don't want to interrupt you in your thoughts, but remember, you promised to visit that poor old man, the one without any legs one of these days. How about tomorrow?" And without waiting for his answer, she quickly disappeared into the kitchen. In his half-drowsy rest, the Reverend thought he heard something about a man without any legs, or was he dreaming about the man with the missing legs? Perhaps it time for a visit to him anyway. Yes, that poor soul will need me.

The Reverend was now fully awake from his little nap. He looked around the room and his eyes rested on the pile of linen. He called the old woman. She burst open the kitchen door and in a flash was by his side.

"We did well today, one hundred and seventy sheets for every church family. Give me a dozen and put the rest in the cupboard, and please remind me to take them to town tomorrow."

'Sure thing, Mr. Reverend. 'Spect you taking the dozen to Phillip's store?"

"Yes. And after dinner, give yourself the evening off," he told her.

"Oh, Reverend, have nowhere to go; will just stay here in case you need me." And she disappeared from the room. In a few minutes she was back with a tray full of extra bread and cheese which she placed in front of him.

"A little extra something for your stomach. You must keep up your strength with all what people expect from you." And she disappeared again behind the kitchen door.

Next morning Reverend Jeffrey piled boxes and bags into the buggy, mounted it, and headed to town. Young boys pushing wheelbarrows full of newspapers called out the latest headlines. "Diphtheria Found in Drinking Water – Keep House and Barn Clean."

The Reverend stopped the buggy, bought a paper and read it. Next he stopped at Phillip's haberdashery and dry goods store and laid a dozen sheets of written verse on the sun-drenched counter. Mr. Phillips picked up a sheet of verse and looked it over before saying, "Reverend, a mighty good revival it was last Sunday. Just what this town needs." Then he paused to read the verse again, "You can be sure I'll point out these to my customers. No telling how these few words will turn 'round a few of 'em."

"Thank you Philip, you are helping to spread the mission of our church. Your shop seems especially sunny and inviting this morning. See you in church."

The Reverend turned and left the shop. He mounted the buggy and continued his drive through the village. People waved and shouted "good morning" as he passed. At a small broken-down old house on the shady side of the street, an old man with both legs missing crawled to the front door and called to the Reverend as the buggy turned into the gate.

"Oh Reverend, 'tis good to see you. Could tell from all the noise and commotion and everybody calling out to you that you was near, so I crawl to the door so as not to miss you."

"Mr. Edwards, I came into town especially to see you, to spend a few moments of prayer with you," the Reverend said, jumping down from the buggy.

Mr. Edwards could not conceal his glee. He looked at the minister with a broad smile before inviting him into the house to hear his life history all over again.

"Come on in Reverend, come on right in and sit right down. Reverend, here I be crawling instead of moving like I used to. Oh, sometimes, I forget I don't have legs. I remember, only when I think too hard on it. If I don't think, then I move about with these crutches, and go to the outdoors and the barn as if my legs are still there. But going further than the barn, no, no. That would be impossible because I would think too much on it, and it would remind me what a cripple I am. Would you believe, I used to be a gravedigger, yes, until the smallpox carry off my whole family. Haven't been the same since."

"Remind me again, how did you come to lose both legs," the Reverend asked.

"Oh, my legs. Well sir, a buggy loaded with pine coffins fall over and pinned me under. Was underneath that buggy for hours before they rescue me. It was the second saddest day of my life. The saddest day of my life was when the smallpox wiped out my whole family."

"And the doctors couldn't save them?" the Reverend asked perplexed.

"My legs, or my family? Well, don't matter. The doctors couldn't save my family. It happened too fast for me to even call a doctor. They were here one minute and the next minute, they were gone. But my legs, no, no, the doctors tried. Yes, they tried hard. Three doctors looked and they looked again, but every time they shake their head and looked me in the eyes and shake their heads again without saying a single word, until the day they took off my two legs." He paused for a moment to fix his voice that was on the verge of breaking. "I can still feel the pain; Oh God. Since then I don't know what it's like to be happy or be sad. The two feel the same to me."

"Oh Mr. Edwards, I've never heard you speak that way before. What is troubling your heart?"

"Oh Reverend, I want so much to do more, to do for myself. If only I had one leg, it would mean the world to me, just one leg so I can move and do more for myself. I sit here day after day and I see malice, and greed, and disagreement, and envy, and hate pass back and forth before my door, up and down the street, and if I could only move and go to town or even to the roadside, I would tell them…" Mr. Edwards choked with emotion and could not complete his thought. Then he cleared his throat and continued. " Reverend, I know so much, so much about this here town and the goings on, good and bad, but…."

"Mr. Edwards," the Reverend interrupted him handing him a sheet of verse, "take this simple verse. Think on it. I hope it will give you sustenance and strength to help you bear the load life has thrown your way." After waiting a few moments for Mr. Edwards to regain his calm, the Reverend continued. "You are not a cripple, Mr. Edwards. Don't think so for a moment. You have a good mind, a kind heart and a willing spirit. Those are traits I want this village to cultivate, every man, woman, and child." Afterwards, the Reverend moved to a corner of the room and put a package with flour, salt, beans, and milk onto the table. Then he said goodbye to Mr. Edwards, mounted his buggy and left.

3

The Reverend returned home from the village, his heart filled with sorrows for the unfortunate ones needing grace. He entered the house and went straight to the sofa to contemplate.

In the meantime, the old woman was on her way from the apple orchard. She grunted as she walked uphill and then downhill back to the church house with a basket full of apples balanced upon her head. Entering the kitchen, she lifted it down from her head and put it on the table. Then she stood for a moment to allow her heart to quiet down. Afterwards, she entered the parlor and stood studying the shabby room. She looked at the threadbare chairs and shook her head. She studied the peeling plaster from the walls and let out a disgusted grunt. Then she quietly removed the pen, ink, and writing materials from the desk and threw on a table cloth to cover the stains and ink marks.

Glancing over at the Reverend lying uneasily on the threadbare sofa, she announced, "Good Reverend, don't forget the Elders coming this evening, and God knows there is little I can do to make the room look good." Then without waiting for an answer, she moved into the kitchen and took four apples, washed them twice to remove the imaginary dirt, and brought them to the table along with a small loaf of bread, butter and cheese, and a bottle of ale.

Just then a hard knock came to the front door. The Reverend opened it and the three Elders entered. With a hoary guttural voice, one of them asked, "Are you ready for the meeting, son?"

Reverend Jeffrey nodded, and the three greybeards, their backs bowed with age, tottered into the inner parlor, pulled out chairs and sat down at the desk. After bowing their heads to say Grace they buttered their bread and began chewing.

"Jeffrey, my boy," said the senior Elder, his eyes examining the ceiling of the room, "this house isn't fitten for living any more. The walls and the roof won't hold out a rainy day, son!"

Jeffrey stopped chewing and answered. "Things are worse than I expected, but I'll make do."

"Then cheer up my son. Remember, King David made his alter on the floor of a barn. So yes, I know you will do well until we can find enough money to repair it. And we will. Now let's get down to the diphtheria business."

"The question is," asked the Revered, "how will we help. Our church families are at risk. Should we go around from house to house and tell them to clean up their houses and barns, boil all drinking water, spread powdered lime around the house..." The three Elders interrupted his speech with a collective frustrated click of their false teeth.

"Jeffrey, my boy, we will do what we can. Next Sunday we will take some time at the end of church service and tell them exactly what they must do: wash and keep towels, sheets, and so on clean, if they cannot keep them clean, they must burn them, and pour oil into all standing water to keep the dangerous bugs and mosquitos from breeding."

"Schools will remain closed, and depending on the severity of this epidemic, we may have to close churches too for a few weeks," said the second Elder.

The three shifted their bodies and silence fell at the table. They ate, and drank, and licked their lips before saying another word.

"Now onto other business, the first Elder announced. "Son you must increase the fold; increase you must. Ten licks to drunks and thieves who refuse to join the church. And whoring women too; you must bring them into the church fold."

The Reverend took a glance at the cat-o-nine hanging on the parlor wall before saying, "Lick the sinners and drag them in, that I can do sir. But the whoring women, where do I find them?"

"Oh, well, we will talk about that later, but now I can hear the bell for evening service going." The men shuffled out of their seats and moved towards the door. At that moment they heard brisk footsteps coming up the path and then a loud knock came to the door.

"You-hoo, you-hoo," came a woman's voice.

They looked out and saw a tall shadow standing behind the curtained door.

"You-hoo, Reverend Jeffrey, It's Mrs. Jeremiah, come to see you," the voice on the porch said.

With a reluctant hand, the Reverend opened the door and the tall figure filled up the doorway. She and her flouncy lavender dress came in and her eyes took a quick sweep of the room. Ignoring the three Elders she turned and handed a basket of eggs to Reverend Jeffrey.

"Reverend Jeffrey, may I speak to you about my sister, Sarah?"

"As you can see, Mrs. Jeremiah, we are just leaving for evening service," the Reverend said. "Much thanks for the gift, but please come again."

As if noticing the three grey beards for the first time, Mrs. Jeremiah held out her hand to greet them. "Oh so nice to see you all. You see, you can help me too."

"What do you mean, Mrs. Jeremiah?" asked the first Elder.

"I have come to speak with the Reverend about my sister, Sarah, and you all can help me convince him she is a good enough girl. After all, I myself am respectably married, so will my sister." Without even the tiniest pause, she continued. "If I may say so, this house is not fit for a Reverend. Just look," and she aimed her fingers at the holes in the roof and walls. "I can see God's light shining right through."

One Elder raised his hand to shoo her away, 'Woman, what right have you to say that?"

A scowl crossed her face, and she opened her lips to say something, but shut it again when she noticed the other Elder tottering on his walking stick towards her, his face a mask of fury.

But she did not relent. Instead she said, "Well I think I was probably a bit harsh. I always say my mind and that is my greatest fault." With all four pairs of eyes glued onto her, she made a resentful curtesy and moved towards the door. The Reverend closed the door behind her, and they heard her slow, reluctant steps moving away from the porch.

"We've got to manage these unruly women the right way," the Elder said his mouth all worked up with rage. "Come my boy, let's discuss what we can do about the house. It's not fitten for man or beast, but we can make it livable."

Reverend Jeffrey opened the door and the Elders toddled down the steps. They moved around the yard making note of the broken windows, the back door hanging half-way off its hinges, the roof and gutters filled with debris from years past. Suddenly they came upon Mrs. Jeremiah staring in confusion at a group of what looked to be runaway slaves standing near a woodpile.

"Who might you be; what are you doing here?" she asked them in a condescending voice.

"Mrs. Jeremiah, these people are no business of yours," the Reverend said. And she turned round quickly to see the four men staring her down. Feeling their scorn flowing towards her, she turned away and without uttering a word, climbed into her buggy and rode away. After the Elders left, the Reverend went to the woodpile to warn the runaways, in the strongest way he knew how, to always keep to the woodpile in the daytime, to stay hidden. "No one must know you are here," he told them.

The next day, just after daybreak, Reverend Jeffrey packed his buggy with small Bibles and religious tracts, and climbed in. He leaned over to make sure the things were securely fastened to the hamper in the buggy, and soon he was clip clopping down the lane to town. He stopped every now and then to hand out tracts to small groups of people who stopped to greet him. Then he stopped at the big store in town where a crowd had gathered and excited chatter reached his ears. His eyes focused on the group, their hands gesturing and punching the air amidst grunts and groans. He moved past them and placed a stack of Bibles unto the counter before speaking:

"Blessings on all this morning." A few guilty looking ones scattered and moved away. The Reverend looked at the still excited group and spoke to them directly, his voice raising itself above the chatter. "Remember, there is virtue in hard work! Why such excitement, people? What is going on?" They turned to look in the direction of the voice. Phillip, the shopkeeper spoke out.

"Poor Johnson over in Heartease, gone to the asylum for six months. The women in the crowd gazed at the ground and shook their heads sadly. "Sentenced just this morning," one said.

The Reverend's face fell into sad folds and creases like the other faces around him. "What on earth for. What did poor Johnson do to deserve this?"

"He stole. That's what he done. Stole money to build a barn," piped in a voice from the back of the group.

"For his starving cows and horses; nothing else he could do, I 'spect," another voice spoke up.

The Reverend raised his hands to quiet them. "Now why did he do something that was clearly wrong, and why the asylum?"

Phillip spoke up and explained. "You see Reverend, poor Johnson lost a lot of money on grain last year with the drought, and the little money he found himself with at the end of the harvest season was not enough to feed neither his wife and five children, nor the five horses and ten cows through the winter, and…".

"So he stole some money," said one cutting off Phillip. 'But the thing is, he didn't use the money to feed his family, or even the horses and cows much. I bet the judge wouldda been a little bit easy if he used that money to feed his starving family, and them animals of his. Instead, he let his family starve, and he let the horses and cows starve some. And then he used the money to build up the broken-down old barn for his animals. Poor Johnson."

"He should'a sold one or two of the cows of his," said one. "The judge said only insane people would do what he done, so they sent him to the crazy asylum."

The Reverend listened, pity and sorrow crowning his face. "We should've reached out to help him."

"Yes, yes, but most of us didn't even know then," Phillips explained. "And even if we did, you know how this town is, every man for himself and...." And Phillip stopped, suddenly realizing the awful thing he was about to say in the presence of the Reverend.

"So the judge sent him to the asylum. They sent a desperate man to the asylum," the Reverend asked again." May the Good Lord have mercy on him. Where do they live?"

As the Reverend spoke, he looked up to see a woman, dressed in black with black veil covering her head and face crossing from the other side of the street towards him. As the woman came close, he saw that she had in her arms a baby wrapped in blanket. The woman came close lifted her veil, spat in the Reverend's face and pointing her finger at him, like a weapon, screamed, "You, you, should have prayed harder. My husband would still be alive, if only you had prayed harder."

Phillip stepped in to protect the Reverend from the irate woman. Taking her by the arm, Phillip turned her around and calmly told her to go home. "Your children are waiting at home for you Mrs. Hale. Time to go home to them," Phillip said in a calm voice. The sorrowful woman stood and waited for the Reverend to answer her, and when he said nothing, she turned and left.

"Who is that distressed woman" the Reverend asked staring after the woman.

"Phillip answered, That's Mrs. Hale, her husband passed on last Thursday from diphtheria. Left her with a baby and three little mouths to feed."

"Oh, the sorrows of our people," the Reverend said pulling a pipe from his pocket and puffing it momentarily for comfort. After some time, he whispered to himself, "Two families I must see on the morrow. Yes, those two need our help and more." Then he turned to Phillip and asked, "where do they live?"

4

While the Reverend was worrying about his parishioners and making plans to visit them the next day, his own family, father, mother, two sisters and two brothers came to visit. When Reverend Jeffrey answered the doorbell that same evening, he saw a sea of big smiles filling up the doorway. When they came into the room, the father asked, "Why the bleak face, son?" The Reverend did not answer; instead he gave them hugs and kisses and helped them bring in bags and parcels of food and gifts and piled them onto the kitchen table. Then the Reverend rubbed his hands together and his face brightened and he asked.

"My face, does it show as badly as all that, father?"

"Yes, I can see distress has found you. What is it son?"

"Sit down everyone, sit," said the Reverend. "God's blessing on all of us," and his arms swept the expanse of the room.

"What is that pain I saw in your eyes earlier, son?" his father asked kindly. As they sat at the shabby desk with its ink-stained runner, his mother put a pile of letters tied up with red ribbons in front of him. He looked up in surprise at the large stack, took up the pile and flipped through them before answering.

"The sorrows of the world are great, greater than I ever knew."

"What do you mean, son?"

A small ray of the evening sun shone through the curtained window and lighted on the Bible sitting on the desk, and the Reverend looked at the ray of light, then over at this family gathered in the room, and he felt the sweetness of the union with them. He stretched his fingers in the ray of light beaming onto the Bible before finally saying, "I've always wanted to be a preacher, even before I knew anything else. Remember? That was the one thing I've always known."

"Yes, yes, son, you've always been a blessing to us. And now you have a church of your own Jeffrey," his mother spoke for the first time, "Don't forget to be thankful for small mercies. You do have a lot to be thankful for."

"I know, mother, much to be thankful for."

As they spoke, the old woman who had been quiet for the last few hours, poked her head through the doorway of the kitchen. She looked around the desk at everyone seated and disappeared behind the door. A few minutes later she came into the room carrying a tray of sliced up roasted chicken, with baked potatoes swimming in gravy.

" Oh, father, mother, all of my favorites foods," the Reverend cried out in glee. He then picked up a fork and kissed it before eating. He ate hungrily, chewing loudly and licking his lips from time to time. For the next ten minutes, those were the only sounds that came and went in the stillness of the room. Afterwards, Reverend Jeffrey pushed aside the empty plate and picked up a letter from the pile. His father lit a cigar and puffed contentedly and waited for the Reverend to open and read it aloud.

"Read them aloud, son. We want to know what people are saying to our very important son."

"Nothing much father, Here is one from the Women's Suffrage Movement. They want me to speak at their meeting. Here is one from the Temperance Movement. They've included pamphlets which I'll hand out next Sunday." The Reverend opened letter after letter. The others are from people asking me to pray for sick family members, for the infirmed, for the dead and the dying. Here is one from a Mrs. Jeremiah. Mrs. Jeremiah. The name is very familiar, but I cannot remember why. Mrs. Jeremiah," he kept repeating over and over.

He opened it and read, "Oh. Now I remember, Mrs. Jeremiah. She came to see me a few days ago about her sister. But why did she send it to my old address?" He looked at the date at the top of the letter and saw that it was written two weeks before he took charge of the village church. He read out loud: "Dear Reverend, I heard you will be in charge here and I want to welcome you to our little community. My younger sister, Sarah, used to be your school mate. Do you remember her? She is all grown up and will be coming to see you soon."

"Ah, she had already written this letter when she came to see me. Mother, do you remember her at all?"

It did not take long for the mother to spit out her memory of that family, "Well son, I do remember her; they are not our kind of people."

"Good God, why would you say that, mother?"

"They are not the kind a minster should associate himself with."

"Why mother? They are members of the church. I must associate with them, regardless of who they are."

"Then, be careful son. Their mother, a certain Mrs. Haggles, she was the one who accused the previous minister of heresy. She might do the same to you."

"Heresy, that's witchcraft mother."

"No, not just witchcraft, in this case."

"What do you mean, mother?"

"The previous minister preached about slavery, that slavery was a bad thing."

"Yes, it is mother."

"Sure, but he also preached that anyone who caught a runaway slave and returned it South to its owners was committing a grave sin."

"Yes, and I would preach the same thing, mother."

"Well, a certain Mrs. Haggles wrote to the church council and all sorts of meetings were called and the minister was cut off and sent away from the village. Now do you see why she could do the same thing to you, son?"

"Now, I see. I see," he said. The Reverend turned his head and his eyes travelled far into the dark, passed the boundary line between the North and South and deep into the woods, and into a little shack that he saw over and over again in his dreams. And inside the little shack stood the six people whose faces became a part of his earliest memories. But the faces faded as his father spoke again, and brought him back to the present.

"Son," he said, looking around the shabby room at the peeling plasters, and at the holes in the ceiling and walls, "this house needs fixing. Why don't you ask the Elders for help. It is their duty to give a livable place to the minister of the church."

"I know father, I don't know how much help I can count on from them. They reminded me that King David made his bed in a horse's stable."

"Rut, rut, my boy, you need a good roof and walls to keep out the cold and rain. A stable it seems would make a better home than this place." his father said, his voice rising in anger.

"Father, I don't know, I just don't know. I want to find time to minister to my flock, to visit the needy, the sick, the dying who at any moment might need grace and guidance. They come first. Only this morning, I met two families in desperate need, both in need of much salvation."

"Yes, son, you are right. Your flock comes first, but a minister needs a good house too so he can administer to his flock without worry," the father repeated. Why don't you ask the elders for help fixing up the house?"

"They have been here, good people that they are, and they know the house needs dire work. But I feel I'm going to have to wait until we have a larger coffer. So I'm going to have to devote time to God, and at the same time worry about getting soaked in a good rainstorm. If that is the life of a minister of God, then let it be so."

"Gracious me, son, you must never say that. You can do three, four things at the same time," his mother spoke up after hearing the despair growing louder in the room. After a quiet pause, she continued. "Son, there is an unfortunate man in Balsam Mountain. He used to come to see us at least once a week. He rambles on and on, something like a confession,

I think. Go and see him. He needs your help and guidance, and your visit will make you feel better."

In his despair, the Reverend tried to respond. He opened his lips but only a gurgle came out. Then he sat in misery and watched as they packed their bags, kissed him goodbye and left.

The next morning, after a wretched night's sleep, the Reverend sat up in bed, reached over and opened the little book which outlined his monthly work. First a visit to the starving family with the father in asylum; next visit the family whose father died of diphtheria last week; next visit the old man who seems to have much to confess. That should take the whole long day, he whispered to no one. He sat for a while and thought about yesterday. He felt ashamed. There he was complaining to his parents about little things that had not mattered much to him before. "No more," he whispered.

Reverend Jeffrey got out of bed and threw open the windows to the morning sun. He picked up a newly pressed shirt slung over the chair and put it on. Then he pulled up his grey flannel pants, jerked the suspenders over his shoulders, and paused a bit to recall the name of the second family he planned to visit. "Hale," Mrs. Hale," he said out loud, and grabbing his hat and coat, he stepped into the kitchen where the old woman wordlessly handed him a steaming cup of coffee. He quickly drank it, packed baked ham, a roasted chicken, and bread and cheese his family had brought him the day before. He then headed through the front door and mounted the buggy to begin the day's visits. After about half an hour, the buggy stopped at a house with rotted roof gables, thin clapboard walls, and tiny windows that barely let in any sunlight. Off in the distance, he saw a sturdy barn, several cows chewing contentedly in the grassy meadow, and horses romping and kicking up dust. He knocked and the door opened slowly and cautiously and a round-shouldered, distraught woman with puffy eyes, and a face drawn with fretful lines peeked from behind the half-opened door.

"God's blessing on you and the family, Mrs. Johnson," he said, handing her a packet of food before entering the darkened house. His eyes soon grew accustomed to the dark, and he made out a bed pushed tightly again a wall. Three small girls sniffled and two boys romped on the unruly bed. Reverend Jeffrey stepped over to the bed and one by one, lifted them off and unto the floor. He led them to a rude table in the middle of the room and taking the package of food still in the mother's hands, he opened it up and carefully sliced off pieces of ham and gave one to each child. Turning to the distraught mother who had not moved an inch from the doorway, he pointed to the chunks of cheese and said, "Mrs. Johnson, I have to go now, but please be sure to feed the children. There is cheese and several meals left on that ham bone. Will you remember to feed them?" he asked her in a kindly voice. She did not answer. She had not moved an inch from the doorway, but as the Reverend walked through the doorway, she took his hand and held it briefly.

One hour later he arrived at a neat little cottage, home of the Hale family. Loud grief met him as the buggy turned into the path leading to the house. Mrs. Hale, still dressed in black with a veil covering her head, sat on a wooden chair underneath an old elm tree whose fallen branches had scattered everywhere. She did not rise to meet the Reverend when the buggy stopped underneath the tree, but gathered up her apron and dried her eyes.

"Hello Mrs. Hale. Let's go into the house. That old elm tree needs to be cut down. A good rain storm might bring it down on top of your head."

"We can't go into the house. I've not had the strength to clean and burn the things."

"Where are the children, Mrs. Hale:

"Gone to my sister's for a spell. I don't want them near this house."

'Good, good, Mrs. Hale, Now let's go into the house and see what we can do."

Mrs. Hale studied the Reverend for a few seconds. She leaned her head from side to side to get a better look at the man she had spat on the day before. Then she rose, lifted her veil and went into the house. He followed her, and for the next three hours, the Reverend and Mrs. Hale scrubbed the kitchen floors and walls, and the bedroom floors and walls with weak lye and lime. Then they burned towels and sheets and old clothes. They worked in silence. Later, Mrs. Hale moved into the kitchen and boiled dishes, cups and saucers, cutlery, and cooking pots and pan, while the Reverend went around the outside of the house sprinkling lime powder into every little crack and crevice he could find. When everything was sparkling clean, the Reverend handed her the package of food and spoke for the first time in three hours.

"I see you have enough wood to make a fire for days to come, but if you should need help, don't hesitate to ask. There are many idle men in town who can come to help. I hope to see you in church next Sunday Mrs. Hale. And, please don't be too proud to ask for help."

When she didn't answer he went on, "God's blessing on you and your family Mrs. Hale."

Later that day, the Reverend's buggy pulled up at a neat log home on the outskirts of town. The Reverend jumped down from the buggy and walked up the steps to the front door. He knocked and a woman who seemed harried and worried, with an unfriendly face opened the door. She noticed his parson's collar and her face brightened.

"Oh Reverend," she called out with much glee, "I knew you would come". And her face changed from worried to placid, and then to holy. Religion glistened in her eyes. I know a little blessing will help him. Thank you Reverend. May the Good Lord bless you always."

She led the Reverend up the stairs to the sick room. Along the way, he heard little bursts of muttering that came louder and louder as they approached the sick room. The woman opened the door to an old man, lying on the bed under several layers of blankets. He eyed the Reverend and called out:

"Good doctor, 'tis good to see you," and his voice was quick and anxious.

"Blessings on you and the family," The Reverend answered. Then he came close to the old man and gingerly sat on the edge of the bed and opened his old tattered Bible. He leafed through the pages and began to read:

"A merry heart makes a cheerful countenance, but by the sorrow of the heart, the spirit is broken."

PROVERBS, Chapter 15.

"What did you say doctor?" the old man asked, turning to look at the face bearing down on him.

The Reverend turned to the old woman who had moved to a quiet corner of the room. Her face had become hard and rigid in the last few minutes. "Has the doctor been to see him lately?" the Reverend asked.

"The doctor been come and gone three times in the last four weeks," the old woman said. The doctor say my man's mind too full of guilt, and only by talking and some confession will the heart be lightened," and her voice was full of relief. "'Tis' good to finally tell someone, so Reverend, if you let him talk, and talk as much as he wants, I'd be much obliged to you."

Saying so, she went and sat on the edge of the chair, her face a mix of concern and relief. The Reverend moved closer to the old man. He bent his head close to the man's face and asked, "What trial is so burdening your heart? Tell the Good Lord and cleanse yourself."

"Doctor, it do do my heart good to see you again," the old man said in confusion.

"No, No, I'm the new Reverend, come to bless you and your family?"

"To speak with me Reverend? Nobody come to speak to me in ages."

"The heart will make you merry, but it will also make you sad," the Reverend explained. "So tell the Good Lord your burdens, and make your heart merry again."

"Well, well, you say you be the Reverend. Well, there is something. Sometimes, I feel like the quiet will drive me insane. It is too quiet, not a voice to listen to. Nobody comes to visit anymore," he went on in a monotonous voice.

"I'm listening; anything you say will be good. It will lighten your heart. Go on. Tell the Lord why no one has come to visit you in a long time."

The Reverend kneeled to get his ear closer to the old man's face.

"Taking me some forty-something years, but I want to do it. Yessss," and the old man dragged out the word "yes' as though it were the one obstacle that had blocked his path for forty-something years.

"You say you be the Reverend?" the man asked again. "Well Reverend, I committed sins against God and man, all in the name of money. Wasn't too kind to my fellow man. No. no. Reverend. Much on my mind these days. Oh, Reverend, I was cruel to my fellow man, and as I lie here in this bed, I can still see the dozens, and dozens of faces I caused to suffer." His monotone was becoming agitated, and his voice raised to fever pitch. His breathing was rapid and irregular. The Reverend lifted his head to check on the old man. He felt his pulse and called out to the old woman to bring water and a cold rag for his forehead. When the water came, the old man drank hungrily and the Reverend wiped the sweat from his forehead, straightened the many layers of blankets and urged him to go on. The old woman took her seat uneasily on the chair again and the Reverend put his ears close to the old man's face again.

"Reverend, will you step over to the drawer there and open it," the old man said, pointing to a desk sitting in a corner of the room.

The Reverend got off his knees and moved towards the desk. He opened the drawer, looked inside, turned to face the old man with surprise, then back to drawer and stared inside again.

"Take out everything you see in there and bring them over to me," he ordered the Reverend.

The Reverend brought over an armful of money and placed it on the bed. Then he went back to the drawer and brought out more armfuls. He brought over piles after untidy piles of paper money and coins and placed them on the bed.

"Yes, all that money just sitting and waiting to be put to good use," the old man announced, turning his head and eyeing the piles of money weighing on his blankets.

He then turned his head and met his wife's gaze. The old woman stood up. She did not look at the pile of money. Instead, her gaze focused on a threadbare spot on her husband's blanket as though she wished it would open up at any moment and swallow the whole untidy pile of money.

"Put it to good use by all means, Reverend," his wife announced.

"Did all of this come from stealing from your fellow man?" the Reverend asked, his eyes growing with curiosity.

"Oh, Reverend, it come from the poor people of this town," and the old man paused to loosen the blankets that were beginning to bind him. To get comfortable, he moved his body from side to side like a snake slithering out of its old skin, before continuing. "It come from starving children, from poor mourning widows and orphans, from hard-working grandmothers and grandfathers, from the infirmed. Oh, Reverend, it wasn't me doing all that wickedness, it was the wickedness I see 'round me day after day that done it, that wickedness got to me and I couldn't resist it. It wasn't me at all; it was just the wickedness, the everyday wickedness."

By now, the old man was breathless with the unusual energy he spent confessing. The Reverend, still on his knees, leaned back to look in disbelief at the pile of money.

"Mr. Gregory, will you tell the Good Lord just how you were able to rob all these people and get away with it for all these years?"

"Oh Revered, my heart is full, and I think the Good Lord is tired of hearing my voice. I can't go on any more, or my heart will just burst with grief."

The Reverend looked over at the old man's wife as though waiting for an answer, then at the old man, before asking in a kindly voice. "Again, what will you have me do with all this money?"

"Give it away to the poor. My guilt says it is the right and proper thing to do. It will set my mind right again."

"I will do better than that. It will feed, clothe, and shelter the indigent and the desolate for years to come."

"Yes, Yes, "the old man said, his voice calm and satisfied. "That will do; yes, that will do."

"Then I must go. Much work to be done." After a pause to put some of the money back into the drawer, and the rest into his satchel, the Reverend offered a prayer." May the Good Lord bless this house and all therein. May

He keep you safe from all temptations. May He guide you through the dark, and give you health and strength in the days to come. Amen."

The old man tried to sit up in bed, but his arms and legs would not let him, and he fell back into the pillows and blankets. "Reverend, that was a mighty satisfying prayer. I do feel better already. I can feel the strength coming back into my body, and I can hear myself breathing again. God bless you, Reverend."

5

On the way home, Reverend Jeffrey stopped at Philip's general store in town. The cold weather had set in, and in the middle of the store stood a glowing pot-bellied stove around which men sat warming themselves while they discussed news and politics. In between, they chewed tobacco and spat juice on the floor. Reverend Jeffrey made a note in his little book to get these idle men together to help him build bits and pieces of the church house. Reverend tiptoed around the wads of spittle and spoke to Phillip. He placed orders for food, clothing, shoes, tools, and bedding for the entire town.

"Yes, Phillip,' he whispered, "every few months you'll deliver these to every family in town. Work out with each family, especially the poor. See what their needs are and see that they receive it."

Later that evening, Reverend Jeffrey had just sat back in a chair in the inner parlor, had just rested his head against the cushions and closed his eyes, when there came a loud knock to the front door.

The old woman raced to answer it, and the Reverend heard the voice of the woman, the woman whose voice had played upon his memories since she first entered the church house a few weeks earlier.

"Yoo hoo, came the voice loud and clear into the parlor."

Before the Reverend could get out of the chair he heard Mrs. Jeremiah enter through the front door.

"Two women here to see you Reverend," the old woman called out from the front parlor. "Spect you want to see them, if not, I can tell them 'no.'" the old woman's defiant voice came to him.

"How dare you," Mrs. Jeremiah's angry voice came through. We are here to see the Reverend, and the Reverend we must see."

Mrs. Jeremiah pushed herself through the open door and dragged her sister in behind her. She dropped herself into the nearest chair and invited the younger woman to do the same.

"No, No, I can't sit uninvited in the Reverend's chair, no," the younger woman answered, respect flowing from her towards the older sister.

"Child, you've got to learn that if you are going to be the equal of the Reverend, you must sit down. Sit down you must," Mrs. Jeremiah's brazen voice came through. As they waited for the Reverend to come, the older sister pulled out a handkerchief from her bosom and wiped her brow. She fussed with her dress, pulling and smoothing and straightening it out. Looking out the window stood the younger woman with her back turned to her sister.

The kitchen noises came to the two women as they waited. "Wonder what's keeping him," Mrs. Jeremiah whispered to the younger woman.

Just then Reverend Jeffrey entered the room, and the older sister was seized with a sudden urge to throw her arms around him and hug him tightly. Instead she calmly got up and crossed the room to grab the Reverend's hand. "Sarah, she called out loudly to the younger woman standing only a few feet away, "Sarah, come and greet Reverend Jeffrey, come child."

A small, lopsided, embarrassed smile came to Sarah's lips, and she left the window and held out her hand to greet the Reverend.

"So nice of you both to come," the Reverend said, his voice attempting to remain calm and placid. Just then, the old woman came into the room to ask the Reverend if she should bring in his dinner tray.

"By all means, do," Mrs. Jeremiah answered, firmly. "We are on the verge of leaving, so don't mind us. Give the Reverend his dinner." Then she turned to the Reverend and spoke. "Reverend, before we go, I want you to know that Sarah won't be in church for the next few Sundays. You see, she'll be fitting dresses for fashionable ladies for the annual dinner dance," and Mrs. Jeremiah's clear, proud voice, with all that it insinuated came through to the Reverend.

"I hope you will enjoy the next few weeks Sarah, and that you'll come to church services when you can."

"Yes, we'll be back around Christmas, Mrs. Jeremiah cut in. "Please come to our home for a visit then, Reverend."

"At this point, Mrs. Jeremiah, I can't say. It is much too soon to think about Christmas."

"Very well then, please keep us in mind."

The two women left and the Reverend sat at his desk, opened up letters, signed two wills and three deeds to newly built houses for church members, and read a note signed by the three Elders:

> "Splendid job, Reverend Jeffrey. Don't give up on the worst of them. Use the cat-o-nine when necessary. I hope these men will do a good enough job on the church house. Splendid idea."

As he read, the old woman poked her head through the doorway. She stood watching the minister busily leafing through the various documents. She felt uneasy. Something hung in the air in front of her, something begging to be noticed, to be talked about, and she must find some courage to do it. After a few moments she went up the minister, stood behind him and tried to interrupt.

"I going to say it only once, if you keep having that trouble-making woman to this house, these here two old knees of mine will carry me as far away from this house, and you never will see me again." And she pursed her lips to avoid saying another word. When he did not look up or answer her, she turned around and strolled back to the kitchen.

Snowstorms announcing the arrival of the holiday season came earlier than expected. It was still the middle of November, and potatoes had to be reaped, and ripe barley cut and threshed, and more flour to be milled at Baker's millhouse and sent to Phillip's general store in time for all the cookies and cakes that were to be baked for Christmas. So farmers in the fields knelt where they stood, and prayed to the Good Lord to hold off the snows until the fields were cleared. And the farmers worked all day and late into the night until all the potatoes and barley were harvested. One day, two weeks before Christmas, Reverend Jeffrey went to Phillip's store to deliver a newly written verse:

> "The Birth of the Coming Redeemer was sent on earth to cleanse us of our Sins.
> Therefore, cease all friction and conflict and sing praises to our Redeemer."

As he placed the linen-clad verse on the counter of the store, he noticed moving around with shopping basket on her arm, Mrs. Jeremiah. Seeing her, the Reverend stopped short and moved to greet her, but she walked away and out the door. Reverend Jeffrey stared after her. He was sure, very sure she had seen him.

"Why, Why did she move away so guilty-like?" he wondered in a whisper.

He thought no more of it, because the holidays had come, and the village store fronts were decorated with bright lights, and red and green ribbons adorned the street lamps. Months earlier, housewives had cut and sewed new curtains for their windows and embroidered new tablecloth for the Christmas table. Houses along the street were dressed up with brightly colored streamers, and lighted candles stood in the windows and lit up the nights. People dropped in at the church house and left gifts of ham, bags of flour, live chickens, and several Holy Bibles for the Reverend. Children, given a week off from school romped in the streets with their dogs. Reverend Jeffrey visited the home of several town families to sing and pray with them. Three days before Christmas, the Reverend received an invitation to come to dinner at the home of Mrs. Jeremiah and family.

That morning broke with a heavy snowstorm and howling winds. By evening it had not let up, so when the Reverend picked up his coat from behind the front door, and pulled his hat far down onto his head, he was wondering if it was worth his time to fight through the storm to visit Mrs. Jeremiah and family. He glanced at the buggy sitting in the protection of the old broken-down shed and was glad he had thrown several horse blankets over the seats to protect it. Pepper, the horse, neighed loudly at the snow swirling around him. The Reverend stood at the window watching the swirling snow. His face in a thoughtful mood, he whispered to the evening:

"I'll go. I must go and get it over with. It is my duty to my parishioners, to all of them." Saying so, he picked up the umbrella, opened the door and hurried out. He jogged to the buggy, climbed in and pulled the reins.

The road to town was quiet, and silent, and desolate except for the howling winds and swirling snow. No other buggies came in sight; no one crossed his path. One hour later, he arrived at the home of Mrs. Jeremiah and family. The windows were brightly lit as though a party was in progress. He tied the buggy to the tree, walked up the path, stepped onto the porch, and raised his hand to sound the doorknocker. Suddenly, beads of sweat washed over his face and neck and his hand fell to his side. A feeling of dread churned in his stomach and he stood wondering if he should knock. Standing on the porch in the storm, he stared at the silver doorknob for several minutes. The dreaded feeling stayed with him. The Reverend closed his eyes to steady himself, then turned around and walked away from the Jeremiah's porch. As he rode home, he wondered what to tell Sarah so she would understand. Is a raging storm enough to prevent him or anyone from leaving home on a visit? He knew his parishioners expected much of him, and she would be no exception. He would just have to be firm with her and remind her of the dangers of travelling out in a winter storm: buggy stuck in mud, horses breaking a leg, damage to the stomach of an over wrought horse, chills and fever, and so much more.

With that in mind, Reverend Jeffrey pulled into the gate of the church house and whispered a silent prayer of thanks for his safe return. He drove into the barn and spent the next hour drying and brushing down his horse, Pepper. Then he fed her, and bedded her down for the night on dry straw, all the while wondering what was that dreaded feeling that came over him at the Jeremiah's door. Was that a warning? Afterwards, he closed the barn door and sprinted to the backdoor of his house. The old woman, sitting in the kitchen on the three-legged stool deep in thought with her chin resting in her hand, looked up at him with questions in her eyes. She said nothing, except mouthed a silent prayer of thanks for his quick and safe return home.

Christmas Eve came and the church house was abuzz with all sorts of noises and chatter. It was the annual dinner to raise funds for St. Stephens's Orphanage, put on by the Ladies Guild Society. All of the important families in town were invited: the Hendersons, The McMurrays, The McPhersons, The Hogarts and several others whose names were not listed as members of Reverend Jeffrey's church, but who had paid twenty dollars to sit with the Reverend for this benefit. The old slave woman worked the kitchen, and the fashionable women of the Ladies Guild moved back and forth from kitchen to inner parlor with trays of baked potatoes, chicken and ham. Then later in the evening, they served dainty little bowls of buttery flan and strawberry cream to top off the dinner.

The old cook wiped her forehead after putting the third batch of flan to bake in the oven, and stepped out onto the back porch to rest her weary legs. As she sat in the dark, she contemplated the two trouble-making Jeremiah women who had not come to the benefit dinner. The old woman smiled to herself; she was glad. "T'will be a good evening," she whispered to the night.

After resting her worn out legs, the old woman returned to the kitchen. The third batch of flan was baked to perfection, so she put them to cool by the window, and began to spoon cream onto the already cooled second batch. She brought it into the dining room. Standing at the doorway of the outer parlor, looking like a small child who was not invited to play, was Sarah, sister of the trouble-making Jeremiah woman. Sarah did not move and the old slave woman stopped suddenly and wiped her face several time to be sure her old eyes were not fooling her. The old woman looked around the room to see if the Reverend had noticed the apparition by the doorway. But the Reverend was busy speaking to one of the ladies. With her worn legs, and her weary arms holding the tray full of dessert, she moved over to the table, laid it down, then with a crook of her finger motioned to the Reverend to look to the doorway. Afterwards, she disappeared into the kitchen.

Reverend Jeffrey lifted his head and gazed at the doorway. He caught a small despair in the figure standing by the door, so he rose and went to greet her.

"Good evening, Sarah," he said in a surprised voice. "So good of you to come."

"Good evening, Reverend. I had no idea there was a party in progress here. Perhaps I will come back another day," Sarah said, her voice full of disappointment.

"No, please stay. You are welcome in this house."

"Reverend Jeffrey, I came to tell you I received your note telling me why you did not come to dinner two days ago, and I came to tell you I quite understand," Sarah said, her voice flustered.

"Sarah, Thank you for understanding. Now, will you please have dinner with us?"

Sarah entered the dining room and helped herself to dinner. She noticed that the other people, especially the well- heeled society women ignored her. So she did not tarry. Instead, she had a hurried meal and left. When the Reverend left the church house later that evening to minister Christmas Eve Service, he realized he had not seen Sarah for most of the evening.

6

Christmas came and went and the little village of Bellville went back to normal. Children walked miles in the snow to get to school, and housewives haggled with shopkeepers and butchers over the price of meat and bread. Four weeks after Christmas, Sarah's sister, Mrs. Jeremiah came to the church house. When Reverend Jeffrey opened the door, she pushed herself in and plopped herself down onto the nearest chair in the front parlor. He looked over at his chair bearing the woman and waited for her to speak. He kept his gaze on her face, and noticed her bosom heaving angrily, but still their eyes did not meet for several minutes. Finally, she spoke in a firm, calm voice.

"Reverend, I've come to speak to you on a very delicate matter."

"Delicate matter, what is the problem, Mrs. Jeremiah?"

He noticed there were tears in her eyes, but through the tears, he could see her eyes were menacing.

"Reverend, everything is far from all right."

"Mrs. Jeremiah, what do you mean?"

"I dare say, you know yourself, that all is not well," she spat out at him.

Feeling a tremendous sense of dread, he fell into a chair in the far corner of the room.

"Mrs. Jeremiah, I am a busy man. Please tell me what your mean?"

"You've been cruel to my sister, Sarah. A minister debasing his own flock. What say you sir?"

Her admonition frightened the Reverend, and for a moment he thought he had stopped breathing. A perilous silence filled the room. His lips quivered with outrage. Seeing her accusation working over the Reverend, her tight lips relaxed. She dug into her bosom, brought out her handkerchief, wiped her face and puffed up her shoulders. While she was feeling gleeful and reveling in her triumph, she heard the Reverend's outraged voice.

"Been cruel to your sister, what sort of woman would make such a claim? Why would anyone make such a claim?"

Mrs. Jeremiah flinched at those words. The Reverend got up, moved closer to her chair and flung angry words at her as he paced the floor like a cornered animal.

"What madness is this, what are you saying woman?"

His voice was just loud enough for the old woman in the kitchen to hear. She pushed open the kitchen door, and stepped defiantly into the room and interrupted the tension. "I'm glad you come when you come," she said facing Mrs. Jeremiah "because them screech owls mighty noisy last night. And the old folks used to say, busy screech owls mean somebody soon going to die."

"Enough, enough, Mammee, no more interruption from you."

But the old woman ignored him and continued, her old eyes bearing down on the seated Mrs. Jeremiah, "So seeing you come here this morning, I know it must be you going to Hell. Them owls never make a mistake." And the old slave woman eyed the Jeremiah woman. She noted her fancy wrap thrown neatly across her shoulders; this woman, all wrapped up in distrust and hostility staring up at her. "But, I will give you one chance to save yourself," the old slave women said. "Get up and get outta that front door now, not later, but now," and her finger swiftly pointed to the door. Then she sallied back to the kitchen.

The Reverend remained silent. He had heard all of those superstitions before, and he knew that many people believed noisy screech owls were a sign of unfortunate things to come.

Feeling the weight of the old woman's words, Mrs. Jeremiah stood up and said, "Reverend, you may rage and rage all you want." Then she swallowed hard to calm her voice. "You've debased my Sarah. You, a man of the cloth."

The Reverend started pacing the floor again. The floors creaked and groaned with distress. His jawbone worked up and down with rage. He lifted his suffering eyes to Heaven and cried out in anguish.

"Dear Lord, what is this. What is this, Dear Lord?"

He turned to face the woman, his face red with rage. He moved and stood beside her again.

"Now tell me again, what is this thing that I've done, Mrs. Jeremiah?"

Mrs. Jeremiah pulled away from him and sat down on the chair again. She fluffed up her big shoulders and stared menacingly at the Reverend whose face was bearing down on her. She got up again and stepped with finality towards the door. At the doorway, she turned towards him and burst out.

"Reverend, you'll pay for this. You'll pay for ruining my little, innocent sister. I'll see to it, Oh, yes, you can count on it." And she slammed the front door behind her.

His chest felt tight and he could not breathe. It was as though the slam of the door had sucked all of the air out of the room leaving him to struggle for his very life. After several seconds, Reverend Jeffrey recovered his breath and he turned to stare at the spot from which the woman had just left. "Was she really here, accusing me of some God-forsaken deed?" he asked himself, uncertain it was not all just a dream? He stared, and stared at the front door, all the while muttering to himself, "Dear God, what did I do?"

The Reverend spent most of the night on his knees. In one hand he held a lighted candle, in the other the open Bible. He read several verses and in between, he asked God what wrong did he commit. "Please God, give me a sign." But no sign came. Next morning he woke to the drip, drip, drip of melting snow from his roof. He looked out on the frosty dawn. It was still dark enough for the trees to appear as one mass of a confused web. As he stood by the window, he heard several tiny scratches coming from a nearby window. He held his breath and listened. In his confused mind, he wondered if it was Mrs. Jeremiah come back to confront him. Then his mind cleared and he realized it was not Mrs. Jeremiah. Was that the sign he was waiting for? He wondered. He listened again and then asked.

"Who might it be?"

"William Penn," came the reply. He closed his eyes and inhaled a grateful breath. The Reverend opened the door to a group of five runaway slaves. He smiled down at them. They were his sign, a confirmation that he was needed, that he was useful, that he was a soldier of God sent out to do good.

At the following Sunday morning service, Reverend Jeffrey standing in the pulpit, looked over at his congregation waiting to hear the word of God. In the two front pews sat ten drunkards he had picked up from the streets the day before. They each held in their hands a Bible, opened to The Book of Proverbs, Chapter 27. Reverend Jeffrey looked lovingly at them before speaking.

"To begin our service today, we'll call upon all sinners to confess their deeds." There was much shuffling of uneasy feet and shifting of nervous bodies, then quiet. From the front pew, one of the drunkards stood up and stepped out into the aisle. He turned to face the congregation and told them about his wicked past.

"I'm one of them who sold his soul to the devil for a bottle of whiskey. I stand before you to ask for forgiveness." Then he read from the opened Bible:

> "Have mercy on me Oh, Lord, for I am weak. Oh, Lord, heal me for my bones are troubled…. I am weary with my groaning; all night I make my bed swim; I drench my couch with my tears…."

And his eyes washed with tears. He could read no further and turned and took his seat. Then without much of a pause, the Reverend stretched his eyes to the back of the congregation and called out.

"Mrs. Jeremiah, you are called upon to confess your sins. Come up here, Mrs. Jeremiah."

The entire congregation turned their eyes upon Mrs. Jeremiah sitting in the back pew. Mrs. Jeremiah, wearing her periwinkle blue dress and straw bonnet turned her face away from them. She drew in a loud breath, and the loud thud, thud of her heart pushed her up from the seat. She stood up in defiance and moved into the aisle to face her tormenters, her eyes alternating between anger and shock. Her shiny spectacles slid a few centimeters down her nose, and she hollered at them.

"What is this? I have nothing to confess. What is this? I have nothing to confess. What joke is this?"

"Come up here and confess your sins, Mrs. Jeremiah," the Reverend's voice came loudly again.

"Yes, yes, confess your sins and break bread with us, Mrs. Jeremiah," she heard voices in the congregation chanting.

"You've strayed from your flock, Mrs. Jeremiah. You've offended the Lord with your quick tongue. Come up here and be washed of your sins," the Reverend called out.

As she stood eyeing the faces turned upon her, her spectacles caught the sunlight streaming through the window. They glistened in a threatening way that seemed to send out shooting darts to the congregation. As they eyed her, she stepped backwards gingerly towards the door. Step by step she moved towards the door. Just before she slipped out, she stopped, her face a mask of fury, her bosom heaving with anger, and war in her voice.

"Lying, lying. You call yourselves Christians, and every day, lying, lying, lying tongues you all are. The Good Lord is tired of listening to your lying tongues. Brimstone and fire upon all of you; may thunder and lightning strike you dead." And with a loud huff she disappeared through the door. The congregation returned frustrated sighs and huffs to the retreating backside of Mrs. Jeremiah. Then they turned their faces towards the Reverend again. They sang the Benediction and filed out in the cool February sunshine.

A week later, disturbing rumors reached the Reverend when he went to town to see the blacksmith about new shoes for his horse, Pepper.

"Bless your heart, Reverend, what can your old friend do for you to-day? the blacksmith asked.

"The mud along Main Street has been hard on Pepper," the Reverend told him. "A new shoe on the left right foot would do well.

And as he shod Pepper's shoe, the blacksmith filled in the Reverend on the latest.

"Spring rains can't come early enough this year, Reverend. The Almanac said something about early rains, but I never put much store in it. I know some people swear by it, but a rainy spring is good because it means more horses losing shoes, and ill-fitting shoes; but just the same I hope it start raining soon." Then he paused for a moment:

"Good Reverend, don't know if tis proper to tell you, but tongues been wagging about you and a certain lady."

Hearing this, the Reverend's heart gave a great thud, but he ignored the thud and turned his head to greet others arriving at the shop.

"Yes, very nice morning indeed. The kind of morning that will make the sick and the dying rise up and take notice," the Reverend pointed out.

"Oh Reverend, you say something beautiful. My wife and me will surely come to church next Sunday," replied one customer.

When they were alone again, the blacksmith picked up where he left off. "That certain lady be Mrs. Jeremiah, queen bee in this town."

"What have tongues been wagging about?" the Reverend asked reluctantly.

"That you be planning a big wedding to her sister, Sarah."

"Oh Dear God!"

"Oh, Oh, Reverend, I didn't mean to alarm you so."

"Dear God, what evil lurks in the hearts of men? Cleanse them of their foul deeds," he whispered to no one.

"Reverend, you have a whole church-full of people who will come to your rescue, so don't worry too much."

"The rumor isn't true and makes a heart full of grief," the Reverend explained.

"We know, Reverend, and no one, no one, will talk of it in my shop. Because I'm going to put them straight. You can count on it, sir."

Hours after going on his religious rounds, the Reverend returned home. As he turned into his gate, he saw a shadow lurking in his doorway. When he got closer he saw it was Mrs. Jeremiah.

"Mrs. Jeremiah, what can we do for you?" he asked abruptly as he came up the steps.

"Reverend, I've come to find out what you intend to do about little Sarah."

The Reverend did not answer then. He opened the door and spread his long arm across the doorway to prevent her from entering.

"I intend to do nothing. Now, you must go. I have nothing further to say to you."

Mrs. Jeremiah took a deep flustered breath. She wiped her eyes and dabbed her handkerchief to her brow.

"Reverend, be a good Christian and do your duty to little Sarah. You know you've debased her."

"Sarah is…" and his voice became even and firm, "Sarah is a member of this church, and I will treat her as I would any other member. I will pray for you both and hope you see the error of your ways."

She took off her shiny spectacles, wiped them several times with her handkerchief, and then put them on her face again. Then she wet her lips before saying:

"Good Reverend, you're a very young man, so I'll be gentle with you. We have a problem on our hands, a problem that we must resolve."

"A problem that I cannot resolve, Mrs. Jeremiah." And he scornfully eyed the woman who had the power to fling his moods to the far end of the spectrum in such a short space of time.

The Reverend turned to enter his house, but Mrs. Jeremiah pushed her way inside.

"You've got to propose marriage to Sarah, nothing less will do."

"My God, what did you say? Marry her, what in Heaven's name for?"

"Because you ruined her. There is nothing less that you can do."

A sob escaped the Reverend's lips and his face fell into a hundred folds and crevices. He held onto the door for support. A hush came over the parlor as Mrs. Jeremiah waited to hear his reply. He kept holding onto the door. He held it tightly, like a holy thing that separated Heaven from Hell, the thing that would give him the strength he now needed to face his tribulation.

"I can't marry anyone," she heard him say. "I'm too poor with debts a plenty, and a house not fit for a wife. The Lord is my whole life, my entire life."

Sensing she might have finally gotten through to him, a small bitter smile crossed her face.

"You'll manage, Reverend. None of these excuses are good enough to stop a marriage. You'll come around." So saying, she twirled around and disappeared through the front door.

Reverend Jeffrey went to bed that evening without saying his prayers. The old mammee did not even come in to see him. She was feeling weak with worry after listening through the kitchen door to the tribulations the young minister would have to face. Before going to bed that night, he had gone into the kitchen to see her, to tell her not to prepare any dinner. He found her sitting on the three-legged stool, and leaning against the cold stove. He was not hungry, he told her. He was full, full of fear, and full of weakness in his spirit so he would be going to bed early tonight.

She looked him over with her old tired eyes. In all her days, she had never seen him look so lost, so displaced, as if the ground under his feet no longer felt firm, no longer held him up. That night she got down on her old painful knees and spent hours, until dawn broke, asking for mercy on the dear minister.

7

The following morning, after a restless night, the Reverend lay in bed thinking about how to get out of the pit he was suddenly thrown into, and how to show Mrs. Jeremiah that she was wrong. In some dark corner of his brain, he knew, she knew she was wrong. But why, why, had she set her sights on him? By evening, Reverend Jeffrey had still not come up with any answers to his many questions. He kept thinking and thinking and then it came to him. At his next church service, he would read from the Bible the entire Chapter 5 of Matthew, the Great Apostle. The "Beatitudes" was needed now. It would remind all those listening of their responsibilities to God, to each other, and to themselves. With that thought, the Reverend got out of bed, wiped the fuzz from his eyes, sat at his desk and began to write his next sermon.

During the next week's sermon, Reverend Jeffrey lifted his voice and blazed a path straight to the back pew of his congregation. But Mrs. Jeremiah was not present in church that morning. Feeling ashamed at being called out to confess her sins the week before, she had not returned to church. But the Reverend kept his voice fixed onto the back pew as though she were sitting there listening to him.

After church services, the Elders stood in line at the church door with other parishioners to compliment the minister on an excellent sermon.

"That was a fitten' sermon, Jeffrey, my boy, for all the trials and tribulations facing you," the senior Elder said.

"Fitten' indeed. But besides the teachings of Matthew and his Beatitudes, young man, what do you plan to do about this unpleasant business?"

"And David said, I'm in a great strait: Let me fall now into the hands of God. But great is His mercies. Let me not fall into the hands of man," the Reverend replied.

"Yes, there are times to leave all to God, but not this time, my boy. You got to do something firm."

"What can I do, short of marry the woman. That's what her sister wants."

"We know that, but not everyone is on your side. Now you must clear your name if you want to continue preaching here," the senior Elder pointed out.

"How on earth do I clear my name?"

"Go see the Jeremiah family. Reason with them. Do what you have to do to clear your name, son."

"Do you mean, marry her?" asked the Reverend, his voice full of fear.

"If that is what you have to do, son; by all means, marry her, but clear your name, you must."

There was a long pause as Reverend Jeffrey absorbed the enormous burden that stood before him.

When he was alone that evening, Reverend Jeffrey took out the problem and examined it from every angle. But each angle ended with a question mark. How could he marry someone who was out to destroy him, someone who had clearly lied and lied and broken the commandments of the church? How could he possibly live in his own skin afterwards? Then he thought of the Bible story of the Prodigal Son and the lessons he learned reading that parable when he was only a boy himself. The older son was very critical of the younger prodigal son who had gone away and spent and wasted all of his inheritance, while the older brother stayed at home and helped his father work the vineyards. After many years, the younger son returned home broke from spending all of his money. The old father was critical of the eldest son for not showing mercy and compassion to his younger brother, the spendthrift, the flawed human being who now needed his family's love and understanding.

So, was that the lesson the Elders were showing him? he wondered out loud. To show love and compassion to all? Even to a flawed individual who had lied, and schemed, and broken every commandment of God?

As the evening wore on, a calm, like a certain light showing the way, came over the soul of Reverend Jeffrey. This realization lightened his burden, but did not completely lift it. He was going to sacrifice himself and his beliefs for the good of the community. He wondered out loud if he had the strength to make such a commitment to God. Please God give me a sign, he prayed that night. And for three days and nights, Reverend Jeffrey fasted, and prayed and waited for a sign. Like the prophets from the Bible stories he loved to read, no food passed his lips. Rain clouds filled the skies and it rained and rained, and the winds lashed great streams of water against the roof and windows. Bucketsful of rain from the rotted roof fell onto his head, but still he kept on fasting and praying. On the third day, the old woman came into the room with a tray of food to tempt him.

"Been fasting too long," she admonished him.

"I can't eat. My heart is full, of what I don't know, but it is full," he answered her.

"Then tis time to go back to work. Babies to be baptized, sick need healing, the dead need burying."

And for two whole weeks, the Reverend waited for a sign from God. He ate little and prayed much. Days blurred together so he could no longer tell when he woke each morning if it was a Sunday or a Tuesday that he was seeing through his window. When he missed his first Sunday service in many months, his congregation came looking for him. They came to the front door and knocked. When no sound came from inside, they moved around the house and peeked into windows and the back door. Their worrisome voices reached the Reverend in the midst of his praying.

"Where could he be? Should we break down the door and go in?"

"Yes, please break down that door. The poor Reverend might be sick, too sick to answer."

"Yes, yes, let's get some men together. He must be inside." And straining his neck to see around the corner of the house, the voice continued: "I can see his horse and buggy still in the shed."

There was quietness for a few minutes while they gathered a few men to help them break down the door. Inside the house, the Reverend was humming and praying, stopping every now and them to listen to the worrisome voices on the outside. The old woman stood beside him, her face grave and stern. Then he heard them bracing against the front door. The little house shook on its foundation, the windows rattled and parts of the rotted eaves crashed to the ground.

"Stop, stop, we must stop," cried one, pointing to a split in the wall. "The house is falling down. Stop, stop; let's stop and think."

The crash of the eaves brought the Reverend to his feet. He stopped and put his ear to the door to listen. He heard shuffling feet around the front door. He heard the back and forth pacing of heavy boots. Then one by one, he heard footsteps moving down the path away from the house.

Two days later, a messenger brought a letter to the Reverend. He opened it and read:

> Dear Reverend Jeffrey:
>
> If you should encounter any more tribulations from Mrs. Jeremiah, this is what we've decided you should do. She must be forbidden to receive communion for a period of six months. In that time, if she does not change her behavior, she must be forcibly taken to St. Stephens Street, to work for a period of one month, to help clean and bathe the sick and the dying. Afterwards, for a period of three months, she will spend time at the Anderson's, and then the Hutche's, and McMurrays farms.
>
> Signed: The Elders

The Reverend smiled a broad smile for the first time that he could remember. Something about this punishment felt right. This punishment would mean all thoughts about a marriage would be derailed for the time being. He felt his energy returning, and he burst into the kitchen that morning and frightened the old woman who was busy peeling potatoes. She quickly fixed a hearty breakfast of porridge and eggs and biscuits and he ate and licked his lips. Later that morning, the Reverend dressed in his church vestments, picked up his hat and Bible, mounted his buggy and set his face down the lane to Mrs. Jeremiah's house.

A strong knock on her front door brought her to the doorway. Her face lit up when she saw him. He entered the house without a word and Sarah, sitting at her spinning wheel, turned her head to glance his way.

"Good morning, Reverend," Sarah called out.

"Reverend Jeffrey, my dear brother, I've been thinking about you. You needn't worry about a home," Mrs. Jeremiah said, as if concluding a long one-sided debate. "You do have a home right here with us." And she moved towards the bedroom and crooked her finger to beckon him to follow her.

"The best bedroom in the house. All you need are some good linens, a few laced curtains and a good reading lamp."

"Impossible, Mrs. Jeremiah, good linen, laced curtains, if that is all I need… " and he stopped in mid-sentence, deciding that it would be foolish to get trapped into her nonsense talk.

But Mrs. Jeremiah was determined to make him see the sense of her argument. " Please be good as to make some sense to me. What is impossible?"

"Mrs. Jeremiah, we both never seem to make sense to each other."

"You will make some sense yet, my young minister."

Reverend Jeffrey paced back and forth as he decided how to point out a little fact to her. Then he lifted his head high and turned to her.

"Mrs. Jeremiah, I did not come to ask for your sister's hand. Please understand that."

"Why did you come then," she spat out. "A good Christian would never say such a thing. I can see the devil is at work in your head."

"And I can see the devil is at work in your head, Mrs. Jeremiah. Mrs. Jeremiah, I've come to ask you to rethink all of those nasty things you've been saying about me."

"Nasty things. How dare you say I lie. Those things are true. Sarah will say so herself."

The Reverend looked over at Sarah who had stopped her spinning to chastise her older sister.

"Sister, you know I don't know what you have said to the Reverend. I have no idea if it's a lie or not. So I cannot say 'yes,' or 'no.'"

"Hush child, be quiet. You don't know what you're saying. Be quiet if you have nothing to say."

The older sister pursed her lips to prevent any more angry words from spilling out. Her eyes, fierce and piercing, were telling him things her lips could not say. Then his gaze met hers and he kept it riveted to hers until a sharp painful cry, like that of a trapped animal escaped her lips. She closed her eyes, stood up and moved to the window.

Not looking at him this time, she hung her head and stared at the ground outside the window as though something out there would give her the answer.

"I want one thing, one thing from you Reverend," she finally said, her back still turned on him.

"What do you want," he asked sharply

"I want you to marry Sarah."

Ignoring her demand, he said quickly. "You must stop those rumors, otherwise I'll forcibly take you to St. Stephen's Street and you will live there for six months."

She spun around to face him. "What? St. Stephens Street?" she asked her voice trembling with rage, then fear. "I'll never go there; whip me, kill me, but I'll never go there."

"Then I'll never marry your Sarah."

Her frown became smaller.

"You must marry Sarah, right away too," she insisted.

"Not until you stand up in church and confess your sins towards me."

"Confess my sins in church?" And she stared out the window again as she contemplated the meaning of that phrase. For a long time she stood deep in thought, then she came and stood close to him.

"Reverend, you can't ask me to do such a thing. That is asking too much."

"Yes, I can and will ask. You asked much of me, and I'm asking little of you."

"That won't be necessary. Once you marry Sarah, the talk will go away."

"You will confess your sins, Mrs. Jeremiah; otherwise, I'll never marry your Sarah."

Feeling weak with frustrations, she moved to the couch and beckoned the Reverend to sit down beside her.

"No, Mrs. Jeremiah, I have no reason to continue this conversation. I've said my piece, and now I must be on my way."

"All right, all right, just one more thing, give me a date for the wedding."

"That will be Sarah's choice, I suppose."

"If the Reverend wants to marry me, really marry me, I'll give you a date sister," Sarah said from her little corner of the parlor.

"Ha. Ha. If he wants to marry you? If he wants to marry you, did you say? "the older sister said, mocking her younger sister.

"Goodbye to you both," the Reverend said. You won't hear from me again until I hear your confession in church. And the sooner the better."

8

It took Mrs. Jeremiah four whole weeks to decide that she was ready to confess her sins. During that time, she thought of nothing else except the image of herself standing before a whole church filled with people she did not particularly like. Her days and nights were haunted by that one thought, until one morning she woke up and realized there was something she could do to soften the shame she was about to face. Yes, she would make her confession, but she would also make amends for her sins.

So that Sunday morning, at the beginning of April, Mrs. Jeremiah put on her black dress, her black hat and black gloves, mounted her buggy and drove to the Olivetti Church. She entered the vestibule and looked around before taking her seat in the last pew. Not a single ray of sunlight came through the arched windows of the church, and she wondered what the cloudy day meant. Was it a bad sign? Should she put off her confession for another day? As she sat thinking, she heard Reverend Jeffrey's raised voice calling her name.

"Mrs. Jeremiah, please come up and confess your sins."

She stood up and slowly walked up the aisle. As she walked, she could feel her back burning with the scorn and moral disapproval pouring from the faces turned upon her. When she reached the front pew, she turned around to face them. She looked over at the women of the Ladies Guild

Society who excluded her from their membership. She pulled up her shoulders, lifted her head and began her confession.

"My greatest fault is my quick tongue, and for that I ask God's forgiveness. There are times when I speak things not true, but there are times when I speak God's truth. To make amends for those untruthful times, I will donate the following to the Olivetti church house: 3 sets of sheets and pillow cases that I embroidered myself, a new rug that I had hoped to put in my own parlor this spring, and an almost new chair so that Reverend Jeffrey will have a comfortable place to sit and write his sermons. These and all of my sins I renounce in the name of God's love."

Mrs. Jeremiah's speech ended and a profound silence filled the packed congregation. They did not know what to make of what they had just heard. "A confession?" Was that a confession?" a few voices whispered.

"This was nothing but a proud announcement of your plans for the Reverend and the church house," a bold voice called out.

Mrs. Jeremiah gave a satisfied heave and turned her face to look up at the Reverend whose face seemed puzzled. Then she turned to the congregation again. When nothing came, she sauntered down the aisle, went through the door and out into the cloudy afternoon.

Reverend Jeffrey watched the retreating back of Mrs. Jeremiah going through the door and he felt powerless to stop her. She had not confessed to the nasty things she had been saying about him. This was no confessional at all. It was merely....What was that? He could not find the right words to describe the things he just heard. He looked over at his congregation, at the sea of faces waiting for him to say something. As they waited, they heard him say:

> "And though I bestow all my gifts to feed the poor, and though I give my body to be burned, and hath no love, it profits me nothing."

First Corinthians, 13: 1-3

The congregation murmured their agreement. No other words were necessary, they thought. The Reverend had chosen an apt two lines to respond to Mrs. Jeremiah's speech. "Perfect," "Perfect," a few voices said. They shook his hand as they left church that day feeling, not pity, but compassion, and a kind of communion with the Reverend, because at last, they understood the conflicts he had faced these past months with the Jeremiah women.

It seemed that June had crept upon Reverend Jeffrey from behind, and it was there before he knew it. One moment he was denying Mrs. Jeremiah the satisfaction of marrying her younger sister, and the next moment, here was June and he was telling her that he needed no help to prepare for the wedding since it was going to be nothing but a plain church service and the signing of the registry afterwards, then a buggy ride somewhere later that evening.

So Mrs. Jeremiah's help was absent from the wedding preparations. Sarah sewed herself several dresses. Reverend Jeffrey bought himself a new hat. The butcher donated a side of beef, and Mrs. Bailey, the soprano, and several ladies from various church groups, helped the old mammee bake a cake and prepare dinner in the church house for the entire town.

Walking down the aisle of the church in his dark suit and parson's collar to stand next to his bride, Sarah, Reverend Jeffrey felt tortured. His parson's collar felt as though a tight noose was strung around his neck. He lifted his arm to loosen it, but the movement made him feel even more constricted. His vest felt tight and bounded his chest like a boa constrictor squeezing the living life out of him. He dragged his heavy feet of lead up the aisle, and before he knew it, he heard the Elder pronouncing them man and wife.

The Reverend and Sarah left the church after the wedding. Groups of parishioners cheered and ran behind the buggy taking them to a little inn ten miles down the road for their overnight honeymoon. The following day, some villagers repaired and painted the roofs and walls of the church house, and Philip's general store donated a new wood stove. The old mammee and a few villagers washed the floors and made up the beds with the new sheets and pillow cases donated earlier by Mrs. Jeremiah. Her new rug sat under the old sofa in the outer parlor, and her chair went into the Reverend's study. After everyone had left, the old mammee stood in the parlor to consider the generous gifts. Then it hit her; she was sure, so sure that Mrs. Jeremiah, that trouble-making woman had planned all along to furnish the church house with the beddings, the rug and the chair. These would be her wedding gift, to be used at a later time when the Reverend married her sister, Sarah. What a sneaky thing to do?

Meanwhile, morning came and the Reverend woke up for the first time in bed with his wife. No word passed between them. The Reverend got out of bed, but did not turn to look at his wife who called out a cheery good morning to him. After a quick breakfast, he spoke for the first time since they left the church the day before.

"Much work to do, Sarah; let's be getting home as soon as possible." His elbow on the table, he finally looked at her, her homely self, wearing a dress of many flowers.

Noticing him looking at her, studying her, Sarah's spoon tumbled from her lips, and she spilled hot coffee onto her lap and had to jump up from the table to avoid getting scaled. She wiped and cleaned her dress, then sat down again. Her face darkened, and she tried to say something to her husband, but nothing came. After a short while, the Reverend pushed back his chair and got up. She did the same and followed behind him back to the room to collect their bags. When she was ready to mount the buggy, he lifted her from the ground and put her into the seat as he would a small child. On the drive home, she held her head high and stiff, and he kept his head looking straight ahead, pulling gently on the reins when they hit a bump in the road, or handing her the reins when he had to stop the buggy and pull the wheels out of a muddy rut.

As they rode home, his head still looking straight ahead, he spoke to her for the second time since their wedding.

"Sarah, tell me two good things that others have said about you."

"Oh, two, only two? I can tell you a dozen things, sir," she said in despair.

"Well for now, just give me two. Later, you can tell me the rest."

"People say I'm kind. That I'm never cruel to beast or man."

"And?" he prodded her

"And that I sew very well. I sew good seams, and hems, and collars and sleeves."

The Reverend was quiet. He did not know what to do with the two little facts she gave him. So they fell into another silence. Their silence was even more so, changing into a brooding quiet that did not invite any questions or comments from each other. After driving for another half-an-hour in silence, the Reverend turned a lack-luster eye sideways upon his wife, as though afraid of looking at her fully, in case he noticed something about her he hadn't notice before.

Then he spoke again. "Tell me what you think of mankind, Sarah?"

"Mankind? Well, I don't know what to say, except that…" and she paused, "the ways of mankind trouble me at times."

Turning to look fully at her, he asked, "What do you mean, Sarah?"

"I don't know, I just don't know."

"Does your sister's ways bother you, Sarah?"

"My sister? Well, Yes, sometimes, yes; sometimes, no."

"What do you mean, Sarah?"

"Well, she's a good person, and just wanted to see me married. And for a while, that was the most important thing to her."

"Anything else, Sarah"

"No, nothing else." And Sarah pursed her lips to avoid saying another word to betray her older sister. And she folded her arms in front of her, and held her head stiff and her shoulders straight, and they rode the rest of the way home in silence. As they neared home, she began to feel wistful. She wanted the journey to last longer, so they could talk some more. She was glad he had opened up and asked her for her thoughts.

When they arrived home, Sarah stood hesitantly at the rickety threshold of the church house. The Reverend, glad to be home, moved past her and went to the parlor. The old mammee came out of the kitchen and pointed to the little alcove beneath the stairs. "Tis all yours now." He moved and peeked inside. It was decked out with a table and chair, his Bible, pen and ink and a small bed.

"Had to make sure you had your own little room," the old mammee told him.

He turned his head to look at his old mammee, and a grateful smile came to his face. Then he entered the room, moved to the chair and sat down to write the sermon for the next Sunday service.

Finally, Sarah stepped over the threshold of the church house and entered her new home. She looked around as though seeing things for the first time. She stood near the threadbare sofa. It looked even more shabby sitting on top of the new rug. Then she caught her reflection in the mirror over the desk. She looked down and smoothed out her bright pink and mauve dress that she had sewed especially for her wedding. Beside the humble sofa, Sarah looked as though she were dressed for the circus. She felt ashamed and ran upstairs to the bedroom to change. A few minutes later she came out wearing a grey dress with a blue apron and headed to the kitchen. The old woman was cutting up apples for a special welcome home dessert.

"If you need the kitchen now and then, just tell me, 'cause God know, this old body can do with some rest," the old woman explained as Sarah lifted lids from pots and pans and peered inside.

"Been cooking all this time, and as I said to the Reverend....." and the old woman mumbled under her breath afraid to finish her thought in case she had already said too much.

"I only half-believe him when he said I should keep doing the cooking," she continued, noisily opening drawers and cupboards in search of something.

"So as I said before, I'm a old worn out ragged woman, and this old body need some good rest," and she turned around and hobbled towards the back porch to sit in the worn-out chair, to give her old knees some sun and her body some energy. One hour later when she returned indoors, Sarah noticed that her eyes seemed more sharpened and her bent back a bit more straightened.

Later that evening, with dinner almost ready, Sarah called the Reverend to come out from underneath the stairs. But he answered as he had done all day."

"Not now Sarah, I have much to do."

"If not now, tell me when," she asked, her voice full of disappointment.

Her husband did not answer, and she disappeared behind the kitchen door.

Sarah sat on the three-legged stool in the kitchen, lay her head on the counter, and wondered how to reach her busy husband. A look of pain and puzzlement came into her face. After a few minutes, the kettle began to hiss and snort and she got up to make coffee. The old woman was sitting in a corner of the kitchen watching Sarah and trying to assess her feelings towards the sister of that trouble-making woman. The pots had stopped bubbling, the kettle no longer hissing, and dinner had already simmered beyond perfection.

"Why don't you call the Reverend to dinner, again?" the old woman demanded.

"He says he's busy," Sarah answered.

"Busy, Lord, too busy to eat? Never," the old woman mocked.

And the old woman wheeled her body around and stepped towards the little room underneath the stairs. She knocked vigorously on the door, and then opened it without waiting for an answer.

"Never in my born days, since you been this yea high, did I never see you refuse to eat. So tell me why you won't eat the good dinner coming out of that kitchen?"

"I will eat right here in this room, mammee. Much work to do now."

Much work now, eh?" She asked in a mocking voice. "Suddenly too busy to eat, eh, eh," and she laughed out loud. Still laughing, she twirled around and left him furiously writing down the lessons he would give during his sermon next Sunday.

For many weeks following the wedding, the Reverend did not sit at dinner with his wife. When they by chance ate breakfast together, Sarah would gently ask him why he was so aloof. And in his sedate voice, he would give her the same answer every time.

"Got much work to do Sarah." And Sarah would swallow hard and remain quiet because she did not know what else to say to him. No longer working at the factory mill in town, Sarah would spend the day sewing new kitchen and bath towels, and embroidering a new table cloth she hoped would be ready in time for next Christmas. Every morning she would put on her thimble, adjusted her needle and thread, and sewed and embroidered all day long. Now and then she would stop to have half a cup of coffee, or tea with strong milk. Half a cup was all she wanted, she told the old woman, because anything more than half- a cup made her anxious and nervous and unable to sleep. At the end of each day, she removed her thimble, threaded her needle for the next day, put her scissors in the drawer of her stool where she would find them next morning, drank a cup of warm milk, and crawled into a lonely bed.

But one morning after Reverend Jeffrey had eaten a hearty breakfast, had licked his lips and pushed himself half-way up from the table to get ready to go on his rounds in the village, Sarah stopped him.

"You're ignoring your wife, Jeffrey."

He stopped short, but did not answer her.

"Do you think God, looking down at us, is pleased with what he sees?"

"God will understand that I'm a busy man doing His work." And with that answer, he drew away from the table and disappeared underneath the stairs.

In frustration, Sarah went to the desk by the window, pulled out a drawer, and took out several sheets of writing paper, her inkwell and a pen. Then she sat down and for the next half-an-hour, wrote three pages of a letter to her sister, Mrs. Jeremiah. Four days later, Mrs. Jeremiah came to the church house to see her sister. She dropped her bags and baggage in the middle of the front parlor, and threw a series of questions at her young sister who had come to open the door.

"What is this Sarah? Why the letter? What is worrying you now? Is your man not here? No?" "No, sister, he's gone to visit the bedside of the sick and dying," Sarah answered.

"Didn't you tell him I was coming today?"

"No, sister. He does not know I've written to you."

"Why not, child. You must keep nothing from him, nothing. Tell him everything, and he'll tell you everything."

One hour later, Reverend Jeffrey returned home and stopped short when he opened the front door. On the sofa fanning herself with a red and white laced handkerchief was Mrs. Jeremiah.

"Come in brother-in-law. No need to be frightened. You haven't seen a ghost. It's only me. Come in."

Without any reply, Jeffrey turned to Sarah with questions in his eyes. When their eyes met, she turned her head away in shame, and headed to the kitchen. The older sister noticed the constraint between husband and wife, but before she could say anything, the Reverend spoke.

"Do you plan to stay with us for long, Mrs. Jeremiah?"

"Yes, I'm here to stay for a few weeks. My Sarah needs me."

" Good God, A few weeks?"

"Yes, Sarah is lonely, says you're ignoring her. Is that true, Reverend?"

"Mrs. Jeremiah, haven't you done enough, enough damage to your sister and me?"

"What on earth do you mean? How can I do more damage? You've ruined my sister."

"Mrs. Jeremiah, you should not be here. Sarah and I need time and space to sort out our feelings. Do you understand that, Mrs. Jeremiah?"

"Take your time, Reverend. You will come to see that she is a good girl, and you will come to like her. But in the meantime, you cannot ignore her. I will not have it."

The Reverend turned around and left her still talking. He took refuge in the little room underneath the stairs.

"Well my, my, imagine going off like that; wondered what I said to offend him." Mrs. Jeremiah said all puffed up like a swollen mother hen. Just then Sarah came out of the kitchen wiping her hands in her apron. She stood in front of her sister who had not moved an inch from the couch.

"Sister, such bitter words to my husband. He is my husband,…" and her voiced died away as she saw her sister's defiant eyes staring up at her.

"Sarah, what are you saying? Are you sorry I've come to help you? Are you sorry? Speak up child?"

"I'm glad you've come for a visit, but only for no more than a day or two. Then you must leave. We will be all right, sister."

"No, you will not be all right. I could tell the moment he walked through that door. You need me."

At that moment the old woman walked into the room to announce dinner. She saw the two women in her parlor and she quickly shut her eyes as if to blot out the image in front of her. Then she opened them again and her old eyes dripped with disdain. She looked from one woman to the other. She opened her lips to say something, then shut them quickly, and pursed them tightly to avoid angry words from rolling off her tongue. Then she turned around and left the room.

"I have one more thing to say," Mrs. Jeremiah said firmly. "From this day forward, there will be one woman in this house, only one woman to look after the Reverend." After a short pause to let it sink in she continued, "that old woman must go."

"But sister…" Sarah tried to speak and at the moment the Reverend walked into the room.

"No, no, no. My mammee will stay, and stay she must."

"Sarah, you do the cooking and cleaning from now on," said Mrs. Jeremiah ignoring the Reverend's demand. "And there will be no more said about that."

"What can an old woman do or say that could threaten you so, Mrs. Jeremiah? Why must she leave this house? Please tell me," the Reverend asked.

But, Mrs. Jeremiah did not answer. She could not tell the Reverend that the old woman would take his side in any argument, and leave Sarah all alone to fend for herself.

There was an oppressive silence during dinner, neither of the three faces inviting conversation, discussion, or dispute. After dinner, they disappeared for the night, the Reverend to his room underneath the stairs, Sarah to her own bedroom, and Mrs. Jeremiah to the corner of the alcove on the first floor. The Reverend, full of fear for the future of his marriage, did not go to bed until the frogs had long ceased their croaking. Instead, he sat upright in his chair in the room underneath the stairs. Sometimes he rested his head on the desk, other times he leaned back into his chair, but still, sleep did not come. When he finally dozed off in the wee hours of the morning, he woke up soon after to the sound of his own voice calling upon God for help.

9

Next morning, Sarah stood in the kitchen arguing with the old mammee. She wanted to stir the porridge, but the mammee would not let her, so they wrestled for the spoon. Sarah was determined to cook her husband's meals from now on. Perhaps, just perhaps, she thought, it will be enough to get him to come around to seeing her as his wife. When she finally did get the spoon from the old woman, the old mammee left the kitchen vowing to return to continue cooking every meal until the good Lord told her, "enough is enough." Sarah ignored her and she cooked porridge and eggs and brought it to the Reverend. But he ate nothing of the breakfast. He pushed it aside telling Sarah he had no appetite.

At that moment, the old woman was busy in her little room off the kitchen searching tied-up old rags that kept her precious collection of things: buttons from old army jackets, and bags with pins and needles she had bent to pick up on her journey through life. She sat at the edge of the bed, and with her chin resting in her hand began to contemplate her life. Should she stay, or should she go? she wondered. Would the good Lord give her a sign? she asked. Later that evening, after the Reverend had again refused his wife's dinner, the old mammee, appeared in the doorway with her bag and baggage, dressed in hat and Sunday shoes. She called out the Reverend from his space underneath the stairs, and when he came out she stood close to him, as though what she had to say was for the Reverend's ears, and the Reverend only.

"Reverend, you been a blessing to me, but I go now instead of fighting with that woman. So until a better day come, God's blessing on you." And she picked up her bags and walked out of the house without waiting for him to answer.

As the old woman walked towards the front door, the Reverend stood wondering what to say to her. At that moment, Sarah interrupted his thoughts with a rebuke. "Jeffrey, we've got to show sister that we can get along. You did not sleep last night, I heard you praying in the middle of the night. Why, Why, Jeffrey?"

But Reverend Jeffrey did not answer right away. Instead, he turned his head towards the road and saw his mammee, her back turned on the church house treading her way down the road.

"I need time to prepare Sunday's sermon. It takes time, Sarah. You know that," he said, turning his head to answer his wife.

"I know, but we've got to show sister that things are ok, otherwise, she'll never leave us alone."

"Why did you bring her here in the first place?" he demanded. "Why did you secretly write that letter to her in the first place. You are married now, remember that?"

"Married Jeffrey? I don't feel like a married woman. So yes, I do forget sometimes that I am a married woman." And she moved closer to him and put her hands on his shoulders.

"I do need time to get used to that fact, Sarah. We both need time."

At that moment, Mrs. Jeremiah came into the room holding a cup of coffee. She rested it on the floor by the couch, and beckoned her sister to come and sit with her.

"Not now, sister, Jeffrey and I have to take a trip to town."

The Reverend looked up quickly at his wife unable to comprehend the lie she just told.

"Why, why are the two of you going to town? Can't Jeffrey go by himself?"

Reverend Jeffrey's humble face became scornful. He looked sideways in the direction of Mrs. Jeremiah's voice, but did not look directly at her.

"If you go to town at all, it should be to the upcoming balls and dinners. You go to town to be with the Petticoat Society," she said, her voice mean and condescending.

"I'll thank you not to question what I do or not do," the Reverend said, turning to face the older sister, his voice firm and forceful. "What I do is of no concern to you."

"But it is. Indeed it is. Everything you do is my concern. Please remember that." Turning angrily to Sarah, she said:

"Sarah, from now on, I will help you sew gowns and dresses for the dinners and balls you will be attending."

"Oh sister, Jeffrey and I don't need such things. If you want to sew, go ahead. I'm sure there are lots of people who will buy your gowns, but none for me."

"What do you mean child?"

"Sew and sell to the shops in town. You are a good seamstress. People will be glad to buy your things," Sarah told her sister.

"No, no! I would never stoop to anything so vile, sewing for other people? Oh, no!"

A noise, like that of a trapped animal escaped Jeffrey's lips and in a huff, he grabbed his hat and slammed the door on his way out. He turned his face towards the shed in the back and reaching it, poked his head in to check on the runaway slaves hidden in the eaves. He looked up and saw several pairs of eyes peeking back at him. He hurried back to the house and quietly entered the kitchen. There on the counter sat his half-eaten breakfast. Adding bread and cheese to it, he wrapped it up and took it to the runaways.

When he went back to the house later that morning, he found his wife getting ready to go to town, and Mrs. Jeremiah reclining on the sofa with a complacent smile, reading a book of Greek literature. She did not rouse herself from her reading to acknowledge him, and the Reverend gratefully passed by and entered his study under the stairs.

Later that evening, his wife came back from shopping in town and laid out her purchases: bolts of calico for aprons and dish cloths, ginghams for curtains, and linen and viols for petticoats. Her sister threw out some hints about spending too much money. But Sarah turned on her sister and reminded her in a harsh voice that every bit of spending lying there on the table was bought and paid for with sweat and tears, and money she had earned and saved over the years from sewing and carting and spinning.

"I've grown up in the last twenty-four hours, sister," Sarah told her, "and I will gladly boast about it every chance I get. I've seen a certain light slanted my way, and I'm very thankful."

"Oh," was Mrs. Jeremiah's only reply.

With the older sister now comfortably ensconced in the church house, Reverend Jeffrey spent very little time in his own home. He found much to keep him in town all day and he took pleasure in leaving the house early each morning, in all kinds of weather, and returning late in the evening in time for bed. One cloudy morning, the Reverend stood by the gate with his buggy; an autumn storm was threatening. He wondered if he should brave the rain and lightning to go on his usual rounds in town. He turned his head to look down the road and the cloudy sun showed off thick layers of mud piled up high from the heavy rains over the last few days. Slowly, reluctantly, he trudged back to the house. With hand on the door handle, he wasn't sure he wanted to go in, so he stood there in the cloudy morning, feeling ashamed that he was afraid of entering his own house. After a while, he turned around and moved to the back of the house. There, underneath an oak tree stood a year's worth of timber waiting to be split into firewood.

He picked up the axe and began chopping. The rhythm was soothing to his ear, and his body responded. It felt free and unbounded. He kept a steady pace, stopping only to pick up the pieces and pile them away. The rain poured down, but he kept on splitting wood. At one point during the morning, Sarah came to see him, dressed in her going-to-town clothes.

"I'm taking the buggy to town, Jeffrey, to buy things I've been wanting for a while."

"But the lane is knee-high in mud and Pepper is liable to break his legs."

"Oh, I'll be careful. No need to worry."

And the Reverend watched as his wife mounted the buggy and turned down the lane. He stood and watched and wondered what was so important to his wife that it could not have waited for another day. As he stood, the sun came out from behind dark clouds and the morning briefly lightened up.

That night, feeling a bit revived from the physical outdoor work, the Reverend got down on his knees and thanked God for his mercies. Then he got up, perched himself on the edge of the bed and wondered about his wife. Why did she go to town? Why so many trips to town recently? He wished he knew the answer. Then he heard himself ask:

"Who am I Oh, Lord? What thing has brought me hitherto? Wherefore, thou are great Oh Lord, for none is like Thee."

Afterwards, Jeffrey fell exhausted in bed. He fell into a deep sleep. Next morning, as he slept, his wife stood over him, watching him very closely for a long time. When he got out of bed later that morning, the Reverend sat in the outer parlor for the first time in many weeks. He looked out at the grey morning coming through the front windows and whispered about needing to go to town to see the sick and the dying. At one point he turned to face his wife and smiled.

"Jeffrey, you're gazing at me. Why are you smiling so?"

"I'm full of the Word of the Lord. The Lord has spoken to me."

"Did he tell you to look to me, not to ignore me?"

Reverend Jeffrey turned his head and smiled at his wife again.

"No. His words say, 'Your enemies will surrender.' "

"Your enemies? Jeffrey, you've become a very fearful man."

"The Lord of Host shall smote them; from the coming of the morn till the coming of the evening," he continued.

Then without missing a beat, the Reverend said, "Sarah, the Elders will be coming to see you over the next few days. Be sure to speak with them. Tell them everything they want to know, about your sister, about our marriage, and so on."

"I don't know, Jeffrey. Why should I tell them our private business? Private things should remain private."

"They are coming to give counsel and to help us."

As they spoke, Mrs. Jeremiah appeared in the parlor.

"If there's a God, Sarah, your husband is a mad man. Ride into town and bring the doctor. I heard him praying all night long."

"When the storm is over, sister. Not now. Sister, were you listening to us a few minutes ago?"

"Yes, I heard everything, so I know your husband is sick."

The Reverend smiled as they spoke, but he remained quiet, his face turned upon them while the two women went back and forth and discussed his madness.

Half an hour later, Sarah grabbed her hat and coat and hurried out the door. One hour later she came back with the doctor. The Reverend was at his desk humming a mournful tune. The doctor walked over to him and rested a hand on his shoulder.

"Reverend, will you stop humming for a moment," the doctor asked quietly. He led the Reverend to the bed and began to examine him. Under his caring voice, the Reverend dozed off and woke up. then dozed off again. When he woke again for the third time, he protested when the doctor asked him if he had been sleeping well.

"Doctor George, I have no need for a doctor; it's my sister-in-law," and the Reverend pitched his head in the direction of Mrs. Jeremiah, "that woman sitting over there who needs a doctor."

"Why do you say that, Reverend?" Doctor George asked in a tender voice. But before the Reverend could answer, Mrs. Jeremiah cut in, her face suddenly misshapened by the anger flowing through her.

"Doctor, I do not need you. He does. Do something about this mad man. He's ignoring his wife, his newly married wife."

Ignoring Mrs. Jeremiah, the doctor spoke to the Reverend.

"Reverend Jeffrey, your wife says you've been anxious and have not eaten well for weeks. What is the matter Jeffrey?"

The older sister tried to intervene again.

"Doctor, I know what is wrong with this man. He is feeling guilty, guilty I say."

At the same time, Sarah let out a hideous scream from the doorway of the kitchen.

"Leave him alone, Leave him alone, sister."

"Doctor, I have no time to praise the Lord, no time to write my sermons, no time to sleep, no time to think," the Reverend finally said.

"But, you must make time for those things."

"I'll make time when I'm dead."

"What a cruel thing to say; why would you say that?" the doctor admonished him.

"Because I've tried everything; I am tired, Doctor."

The doctor beckoned to Sarah to come near. She left the doorway of the kitchen and came to him. The doctor moved close and whispered. "See that he gets lots of rest. No physical work, no worries, no miseries, no anxieties."

The doctor looked around the room and beckoned to Sarah to come even closer.

"Is there something, or someone causing your husband's misery?"

"Yes, my sister wants the best for me, so she's very hard on him."

"Well, he's your husband; do make sure that he gets well." The doctor paused and looked at Sarah in a critical way.

"And see that you too get some rest."

Sarah held the doctor's arm in a possessive way and led him to the front door.

Later, she looked in on her husband and tucked him in for the evening.

Three days later, the Reverend's appetite had still not returned. He was still visibly agitated and his restlessness was the last thing his wife soothed before she tucked him in at night, and the first thing she confronted when she woke each morning and went to look in on him. Then slowly, the Reverend found himself trying to eat again. The three of them ate together the meals Sarah prepared. Sarah sitting quiet and thoughtful at the dining table, the Reverend staring at the wall and picking at the food on his plate, and Mrs. Jeremiah lapping up the stew and licking her lips afterwards.

One morning as the Reverend sat staring at the kitchen door, he suddenly jumped up from the dining table, ran to the room underneath the stairs and grabbed his church vestments. No one looked up as he moved through the house gathering up his Bible, his sermons and other church things and headed through the back door. In one quick moment, he was standing by the wood-pile staring at the pieces of firewood he had cut a few weeks earlier. Before he could think about it, he felt his hand taking a spear of wood, lighting it and throwing it onto the pile. Then a powerful urge came over him to throw down his vestments. And in one quick movement, he looked down and saw his robe, his stole, his maniple, his Bible and reams of sermon going up in smoke. A bitter smile crossed his face and he called out.

"To the enemies of the night, light them up."

Meanwhile, Sarah, still sitting at breakfast lifted her head and sniffed the air.

"Smoke, is that smoke? Oh Dear God, it is smoke." And she pushed back her chair and ran to the back door. There she saw her husband, the Reverend, staring at the flaming pile of his life's work.

"Jeffrey, Jeffrey, what is this?" she screamed at the top of her voice. And she gingerly approached the pile of burning things. She stooped down and looked into the pile. Familiar pieces of his robe, of his Bible, of his life smoldered in the pile. Sarah got up and rushed to the kitchen to get water and for the next hour, she and her sister doused the flames that would not die. Afterwards, Sarah led the Reverend to the study and covered him with blanket. Then she went downstairs and confronted her sister.

"Sister, time for you to go home. Time enough, sister."

Mrs. Jeremiah did not know what to say. She sat tapping her fingers on the table, and wondering if her sister might be right. Is it time to go? And leave her all alone with this madman? At a time such as this to leave? No. No.

"Oh, no, Sarah, I won't go. You need me, more now than ever. You will need help with your husband. I could never think of leaving you alone to care for that burden."

Sarah did not try to argue with her sister. Instead, she went to the desk, pulled out paper, pen and ink, and wrote a letter to her sister's husband begging him to come and get his wife.

The following morning as Reverend Jeffrey rested in bed, Sarah answered a knock at the front door. She opened it to see the three Elders of the church, their faces grave and full of concern. They entered the parlor, and the first Elder abruptly asked for the Reverend.

"Where is he?"

"Still in bed, getting needed rest," Sarah answered, flustered.

"Still in bed? It's ten o'clock. Doesn't sound like the Reverend, lazing in bed so late in the day? Take us to him."

The three followed Sarah to the room underneath the stairs. They found him curled up underneath a bundle of unruly sheets, his sad eyes looking out on what probably seemed to him a disappointing world.

"Jeffrey, we've come to speak to your wife, but won't do so unless you're present. So get up young man and get your day going."

"To speak with me, to speak to me?" Sarah asked with much alarm. "I'm not ready to speak to you, please not today."

Hearing this, the Reverend jumped out of bed and confronted his wife.

"Sarah, I told you weeks ago to expect the Elders. So yes, you must speak with them today."

"Young woman, do not waste our time," the first Elder warned. "Your husband says you've been difficult and I can see that. We are here to remedy that."

"Oh, Oh."

She led them out of the bedroom, and into the parlor. Each Elder pulled out a chair from the dining table and they sat in a semi-circle. They beckoned to Sarah to sit in the empty chair in the middle of the group. Hearing the commotion, Mrs. Jeremiah pushed her head half-way around the corner of the stairs, and seeing the Elders, uttered a quick "Oh!" Her mocking voice reached them before she disappeared behind the alcove. They looked up just as her back disappeared around the corner.

Then they turned their attention to Sarah.

"We want to hear from you, in your own words, before we passed judgement," the first Elder said. Tell us about life with the new minister, life with your new husband."

Without as much as a pause, Sarah said, "My husband says he's too busy to spend time with me. Says God and the church come first, last and always."

"Well said, yes, first, last, always, well put," one Elder replied.

"Do you disagree with your husband? Do you think you should be first in his life, and everything else, later?"

"I don't know. I do want to be amongst the important things in his life," she said, with a grateful sigh, at last beginning to feel comfortable with them.

"But you are important, my child. You are the minister's wife, a pillar of society. What more do you want?"

"To feel like a wife!"

"Oh, no. No one can do that for you, but you. You are the only one who can make yourself feel like a wife. So, stop whining. Look to your husband. Give him healthy foods, teas, soups, and victuals to make him well again."

"But I do that already."

"You're doing too little, young woman. When you've done enough, you'll feel like a wife. Now, attend to your husband."

Sarah remained seated. "Attend to your husband now, look to your husband now," the words kept echoing in her head. The Elders stood up and waited for her to leave. As she sat there defying their orders, she heard one of them say"

"Child, you're being vain, and vanity is a sin against God."

"No, not vain, not I," she said, her eyes pleading for sympathy.

Their gaze stayed with her, patiently waiting for her to go to her husband.

Then she heard one of them say, his voice full of authority, "we'll consult with the Lord and your punishment will be swift."

Sarah finally stood up and straightened her shoulders. She did not go to her husband then, instead she turned towards the kitchen. The Elders put their heads together, whispered, and chuckled, then whispered again.

"Bring your sister to us," one Elder called out.

She passed through the parlor on her way up the stairs to bring her sister. She did not look at them, but they looked at her and wondered why was she so quick to get her sister, yet so slow to go to her husband who needed her help.

A few minutes later, Sarah and her sister stood reluctantly before the Elders. Mrs. Jeremiah, looking ruffled and agitated shook her head several times. Then she addressed the Elders.

"What is this? Summoning me as if I were a mere servant!"

"You have both broken the vow of good, civilized, caring women."

"Vow? I've been nothing but good and caring. Why do you think I'm here?" Mrs. Jeremiah spat out.

"I've seen you firsthand. You're a perverse woman," the Elder pointed out. "You fear neither God nor man. And fear, my dear woman, is the beginning of wisdom."

And without giving her a chance to respond, he went on. "The punishment to both of you will be as follows:"

"Punishment, did you say punishment, dare you say punishment to me?"

'Now, you will go to St. Stephens Street and offer your help, then unto the farms to help bring in the grains."

"St. Stephen's, did you say…."Mrs. Jeremiah tried to interrupt, but the Elder continued even louder, drowning out her voice.

"…then unto the families in town with five or more children. You will help clean barns, houses, and outhouses before the cold weather sets in, for a total of six weeks. Now, is that clear?"

"How can I do all that and still care for my husband?" Sarah asked in an injured voice.

"Oh, you will help all right; being out of this house will be the greatest help, young woman."

Sarah dropped onto the couch and covered her face. Loud sobs poured from her heart.

"I won't do such a thing, no, you can't punish me. I've done nothing to deserve punishment."

Mrs. Jeremiah's sharp tongue rebuked them." There you stand telling me what I should do with my time, my own time, how to spend my precious time. How dare you?" she repeated.

"We will see, good woman, we will see."

10

After the Elders left the church house, the three did not speak to each other. The sisters moved around the house, solemn and quiet as though death had visited. The Reverend did not leave his room underneath the stairs, and the kitchen stove stayed quiet and cold all day.

Two mornings later, the Reverend heard a gentle voice waking him from a groggy sleep.

"Time to get up Jeffrey, time to wake up."

When he opened his eyes, a familiar face came into focus. "Oh mother, you are here, Why?" he asked, his eyes confused by her presence in the house.

"The Elders wrote to me son. I came right away."

"Oh mother, what time is it; how long have I been sleeping?"

"You've been asleep for 18 hours."

"Eighteen hours, My Heavens. I do feel groggy, but very restful?"

"A hearty breakfast awaits you, son. Get up and get some food into you."

After gazing lovingly at his mother, he said, "two days ago, then today must be Friday. And Sarah and her sister have gone to St. Stephen's Street."

"Yes, the house is quiet, and I'm here to help you."

Reverend Jeffrey pulled himself up slowly out of bed, moved gingerly to the desk and pulled out a drawer. There he took out an old tattered Bible, lifted it to his lips and kissed it.

My old Bible," he said, turning to his mother. "My first Bible, and the best of the three remaining ones I have."

"Remaining, only three remain?"

"Yes, I destroyed a few of them some weeks ago. I regret it now, but God knows… I…Oh mother, so good of you to come." And Reverend Jeffrey opened up his arms and hugged his mother tightly.

She stepped back and looked up into his face. Worrisome questions came to her lips. Your Bibles? Why did you destroy them, she wanted to ask. But instead she said, "Son, your breakfast, you must be hungry."

"I'm hungry for food, but also for something else."

"The Word of God?" she asked knowingly.

"Yes, the Word."

After a hearty appetite, Jeffrey leaned back on the couch and read the latest newspapers his mother had brought from town. He read a few of them aloud while his mother prepared dinner.

"{$7,000 in settlement for a passenger who died in the Vermont-Canada railroad explosion back in 1855}"; and, "imagine this: {a small town in Kansas, only four years old, name of Leavenworth, has a population of 10,400, with nine churches, ten schools, four daily

Newspapers, four weekly newspapers, seven printing offices, eighty-nine lawyers, and forty doctors.}"

"All for 10,400 people, you should feel jealous. Jeffrey, how many lawyers do we have here in this town?" his mother asked.

"Two lawyers, and three churches, and two doctors who serve as vets, two schools, and perhaps two thousand population. Very interesting indeed. I do feel jealous."

The Reverend continued to leaf through the newspapers while his mother kept busy in the kitchen. For a while the only sounds in the whole house was the clock ticking on the mantle and the Reverend flipping through the newspapers.

After dinner, Reverend Jeffrey sat at the desk to write the next week's sermon. As he wrote he tapped his pen and thought of his trials of the last few weeks. His memories took him back to his first sermon, and he decided he would deliver it again next Sunday, word for word, to remind himself of the wonders of God's teachings. As his mind drifted backwards to the early days of his ministry, the sound of footsteps dragged him back to the present. Familiar noises were coming up the path. He drew a breath and listened.

"Who could that be," his mother asked from the doorway of the kitchen. As mother and son listened, the door flung open and in came Mrs. Jeremiah and Sarah.

"Not one word, not one word from either of you," the older sister said, her eyes raking over Jeffrey's mother as if looking for answers to her presence in the house. "We belong here, not at St. Stephen's Street."

The six weeks of punishment lasted exactly two days. Sarah and her sister, and the Reverend and his mother moved through the house with silent scorn towards each other. Neither one wanted to take the first step to leave the house to the newly-weds. They each felt they had reason to be there. So they avoided being together in the same room as much as possible, except in the kitchen. Only at dinner time did they come together, finding it easier and more efficient to prepare a meal and eat it together. The first evening they had dinner together, the Reverend almost choked on his chicken leg when he tried to swallow and found his throat had closed up with distress.

The following evening as Mrs. Jeremiah chewed her buttered bread, she tasted a foul sensation moving over her tongue. She spat out the bread quickly and noisily and those at the table looked up.

"Hell, what bitter thing is this?" she asked, her voice demanding an answer.

A mild flash of anger crossed Sarah's face and the bean soup almost choked her when she tried to reply. "There is nothing on the bread but butter. You saw me put butter on it, sister; why do you ask such questions?"

"Because it tastes foul; why shouldn't I ask such questions?"

"You're just being hard again, sister, for no good reason," Sarah said, taking a bite of it herself and savoring the taste. "No bitter taste at all, sister; just plain fresh butter."

"Ahhhhgggg," she replied. There was an uneasy pause as Mrs. Jeremiah tore off small pieces of bread and began to chew again. The discomfort showed as her eyes dolefully shifted from the Reverend, to his mother, and then to Sarah. A few minutes later, Sarah got up and started clearing away the dishes. She washed and dried and put them away, then, she dried pots and pans and stacked them in the cupboard. Afterwards, returning to the dining room she found her sister sitting alone, a flushed look on her face. Her breathing was shallow, like someone who had just run a hundred miles.

"My eyes are quite heavy. I think I'll go to bed early," the older sister said, her voice low and humble.

"So early sister? Are you not well?" Before she could finish her question, her sister's head fell onto her chest and she was already fast asleep. She lifted her sleeping sister and led her to the couch, covered her with a blanket and left her to sleep. Later that evening, Mrs. Jeremiah tottered into the kitchen, her head resting sideways onto her shoulder, and her eyes seeming to bulge out of her forehead. She was muttering, "Dear Lord, Dear Lord."

Sarah quickly dried her hands in her apron and stood near her sister, "What is it sister?"

"Dear Lord, I don't know. My eyes feel like they are swimming in my head."

"Perhaps we should get the doctor," Sarah said, her voiced full of concern.

"Yes, child. I have a headache, a pain as big as this," she said, opening her hands wide. "I don't feel well at all."

Sarah led her sister to the bedroom, but before they reached the doorway Mrs. Jeremiah collapsed to the floor. Her loud thud sent the Reverend and his mother quickly into the room.

"What is this, what is this?" the Reverend asked, wondering why the vibrant woman of this morning seemed to be fading away in front of him. He bent down and listened to her breathing. It was shallow, so he got up, rushed to the barn, mounted his buggy and rode into town to get the doctor. In the meantime, Sarah stood watch over her sister. She bent her head and listened several times; each time her breathing seemed fainter and fainter. The doctor came, examined Mrs. Jeremiah, shook his head several times, and then pronounced her dead.

Sarah knelt on the floor and stared at the body of her sister. She wanted to ask the doctor how and why, but her tongue stuck like glue to her mouth and no words came out. The fear that her sister was gone in a flash, in the blink of an eye, disturbed her. She trembled and her lips quivered. A strange mood had come over her, a kind of rage. She felt the urge to scream to ask the Heavens, why? But even the scream died on her tongue. Nothing came. She felt paralyzed. She called out her sister's name, "sister, sister," even though she expected no answer.

News of the death of Mrs. Jeremiah roused the village, and in the fading daylight they came, and kept coming to the house to mourn. Frightened villagers discussed the Reverend's bad luck. The church house was now a dead house, they said, and they wondered if his coming to town was the beginning of some kind of calamity for them and their families. Never in the two-hundred-year history of the town had anyone died in that house, they said.

Sarah had recovered from her fright soon enough to realize her sister needed her. So she hastily sewed together a shroud, washed her sister's body and anointed it with clove and peppermint oils, and wrapped it in the shroud. Then she placed the body in the room underneath the stairs to await the coffin that the Reverend had ordered that evening. Afterwards, she lit a candle and placed it beside the body of her sister, and she and the Reverend's mother knelt and prayed for the soul that had no time to beg for forgiveness of her sins.

Sarah wept and prayed several times an hour over the next few days. Doctor George performed the autopsy and wrote long scribbles in his notebook. And the body of Mrs. Jeremiah was interred in the church cemetery in the presence of family and a few dozen curious villagers.

A week after the burial, the church house tried to get back to normal. Reverend Jeffrey's mother packed her bag, mounted the buggy and her son drove her home to Beholding. With his mother and Sarah's sister no longer in the house, the Reverend and his wife began to spend more time together. Every morning at breakfast, they had the same exact conversation, each telling the other what they would do that day, how good the breakfast was, and whether it would rain or shine. At the end of each day, they discussed the same things all over again. Sarah started sewing and embroidering again.

One morning the Reverend looked up from writing his sermon to the sound of his wife's voice. She was threading her needle, her sewing kit balanced on her knees, and the red and white table cloth was beginning to take shape. She looked up from her sewing and told him she wanted to ride into town with him that day. He noticed her voice was pleasing, not the fearful, dull voice he had come to know since their wedding.

"And afterwards, in a day or two, we can begin to do some of the things we've not been able to do," she said. Not waiting for him to answer, she went on. "We are alone, Jeffrey, alone. It was nice of your mother to come, but now we are alone."

"Well I must admit, my heart feels lightened and unburdened," he told her. "But tell me, what sorts of things should we do now that we are alone?"

"Well, such as having a honeymoon."

"No, no, I can't leave church business now, not at all."

And then he turned on her. "Sarah, you should be mourning your sister, not celebrating as though nothing has happened." The Reverend watched his wife's gleeful face, like a child expecting a special treat. Her glee did not change. She seemed unburdened by life's cares and concerns, and a dark troubled look came to the Reverend's heart and stayed there.

11

It was early autumn in the village, and every able-bodied person was needed to help the farmers bring in the barley and wheat. From early morning until long after dusk, Reverend Jeffrey and everyone over the age of twelve, rode wagons and buggies from farm to farm to help cut and thresh the wheat. As the Reverend was getting ready to leave one morning, the dogs on the back porch began to bark loudly. Sarah came down the stairs to complain about the barking dogs. Reverend moved to the back porch to quiet them, and there he found Phillip, the shopkeeper.

"Ah Phillip, what gives so early on a Saturday morning?"

"Ah Reverend, I couldn't wait to see you in church tomorrow, couldn't wait at all."

"Why Phillip, what is the matter?"

"It's about your missus." And he paused to let it sink in. "Your missus buy some poison from me weeks ago, say it was for rats. There's been whispers going on…" Phillip stuttered as he tried to find the right words. "Whispers that she going to use it on you, so I just come to warn you, especially since her sister gone under dark clouds."

"Oh Phillip, thank you, but Sarah did not poison her own sister. Mrs. Jeremiah died of the stroke. God bless you Phillip, for telling me."

"Ah yes," said Phillip, nodding his head. "She was the kind to die of a stroke. Thank God I was wrong. Better be wrong now, than find out later I was right. See you in church then, Reverend. Glad I was wrong."

But Reverend Jeffrey was troubled. After Phillip left, the Reverend stood on the porch for a long time before entering the house, thinking and worrying, with Phillip's words echoing in his head. "…she's going to use it on you."

When he entered the house later, Sarah was sewing in the parlor. "Why did the shopkeeper come to see you, Jeffrey?" Sarah asked. "I noticed he didn't bring feed for the horses, so why?"

The Reverend paused before he answered. "He hadn't seen me for a while, so he came to check that all was well," and Reverend Jeffrey lied for perhaps the second time in his life.

"Jeffrey, I hope it's not too early to bring up this, but sister has been dead for two months now, and I see no change in you towards me; why Jeffrey, why?"

"I'll still be going to town for the next three weeks or so, Sarah. The farmers still need help bringing in the harvest. Perhaps you too can come, Sarah?"

"No, No, I could never do that; you know I couldn't." A wave of disappointment straggled her voice. Then she found her voice and continued: "What kind of a wife do you think I am?"

"A minister's wife who takes an interest in helping other people."

"Oh, so the Hendersons and McPhersons, McMurrays, the Andersons and the fashionable ladies will laugh behind their hands at the minister's wife digging potatoes."

Ignoring her, the Reverend went on. "After three more weeks with the farmers, if I'm needed, I'll help the butchers kill hogs and sheep; I can gut a sheep, you know. I might even shear some sheep too. So you see, Sarah, there is much work to be done."

"Stop, stop! I'm tired of hearing about all the work to be done," and Sarah tried to cover her ears from the work, work, and more work that assaulted her senses. "I am the minister's wife," she said, her voice becoming louder and louder. "I'm the minister's wife, not someone to be laughed at."

"Yes, you are the minister's wife. Please do not forget that."

"And you should not forget that too, Jeffrey," she said, her defiance piercing the air.

Several weeks went by and the Reverend worked the farms, the slaughterhouses, and dipped and sheared sheep. At the end of each day tired and worn, with aching back and tired arms and legs, he entered the house, said "good evening" to his wife and went straight to sleep. Some nights, in the middle of deep sleep, he would suddenly leap up from the bed because he would remember he had not fed the runaways hiding in the barn loft. And he would quietly get up, tip toed to the kitchen, pack up the uneaten food, silently open the kitchen door and sprint to the barn. Without a word, he would push the packet through the opening to them. Then quietly return to the house without making a sound.

One morning, as Sarah was measuring out her usual tiny half cup of coffee that kept her anxieties in check, she called out to her husband who was passing through the kitchen on his way to the buggy.

"Are you fasting, Jeffrey? You've not eaten in days and days."

Phillip, the shopkeeper's words kept ringing in his ear. Every time he entered the house, the words, "your missus buy rat poison - to use on you." confronted him.

Reverend Jeffrey wanted to tell her that he knew she had bought rat poison, but he didn't know how. Perhaps, the Good Lord will give him a sign. So instead he answered: "Yes, Sarah, the Elders have said that for a whole year I must fast from time to time. That is my way of remitting my sins, in case I unknowingly caused your sister's death. So sometimes I do eat, sometimes not," he lied for perhaps the third time in his life.

Reverend Jeffrey found himself becoming anxious about his wife's ability to poison him. Would she put it in his meals? He wondered about it every little spare time he had. So every Sunday, his sermon was put directly into her ears with the hope she would come to him and unburden her soul. He preached about living a high moral life, about the value of hard work, the love for one's neighbors, about compassion for the sick and infirmed and for widows and orphans. Each and every one in his congregation had a role to play in life, he admonished them, a role that fits God's will and God's teachings. His followers often left church service feeling cleansed and ready to do God's bidding. "Thank you, Reverend," or "A mighty, mighty, good sermon that was," or "I feel full of thanksgiving, Reverend," they often said when they shook his hand on the way out the church door.

"Go out and do good," the Reverend often replied.

But Sarah remained quiet. Not a single word left her lips. The Reverend was tempted several times to rummage through the house in search of the rat poison, but each time he looked when Sarah went to town, she could tell he had been searching for something when she came back. "Why is my neat pile of dish towels so ruffled up?" or "I'm sure I left the cupboard door locked," or "why is my basket on the floor and not on the counter?" Eventually, he stopped searching. 'I'll leave it in the hands of God, he whispered one night when the temptation came especially strong and fast and would not leave him alone. But he kept a watchful eye on Sarah, making excuses to leave the house whenever she offered a meal. But with his responsibilities to the farmers over for the season, he no longer had many excuses left. So they occasionally sat in the parlor together after the evening fires were lit and the house had become warm and cozy, and discussed the goings on in the village. One evening, Sarah brought something out of the desk drawer and held it out to him.

"A gift for you, Jeffrey," she said.

He took the leather thing, turned it over several times before asking her what it was. "A cover for your Bible," she said. He lifted it up to the glow of the fireplace and examined it.

"Very fine stitching, Sarah, and a nice strong vein for the back. This should last me a very long time." Then she came and sat beside him, like a devoted wife, and he turned his head and gazed in her eyes.

"This is a very thoughtful gift, Sarah. Thank you very much."

If she took the time to sew me such a lovely gift to be used for many, many years, then perhaps I should stop wondering if she is capable of poisoning me, he thought to himself that evening. Over the next few days, the same thought kept coming back to him - she gave me a Bible cover that is meant to last forever. A few days later, no longer feeling so threatened by the thought of poison lying somewhere in the house, he began to compliment her on her cooking. They now spent more time together in the parlor mornings and evenings and sometimes in between after lunch. The Reverend sometimes wrote his sermon from the little desk in the parlor, and sometimes he asked Sarah to cut up the small pieces of linen so he could write little verses for his congregation. But they never held hands, or embraced each other, and they went to bed in separate rooms. One morning as the Reverend was getting ready to do his daily rounds in the village, Sarah confronted him.

"Jeffrey, let's go away, now that fall is here. Let's take a weekend away together. The Elders will understand."

"Why, Sarah. You've been so good not bringing this up for a while. I was beginning to think you have finally understood how difficult it is for a minister of the church to find time for anything but church business," he told her calmly. "We can't do it, Sarah."

Sarah did not answer. That night in bed she turned her head and faced the blank wall. Cruel tears flowed down her cheeks and her heart opened up and poured out the pent-up feelings of the last few months.

For the next few days, she did not speak to him. When he said he was leaving to go into town, she did not reply. After he left, she would sit at the dining table and pour out her half cup of coffee. She would drink it slowly, her mind wandering upon all the things she would do that day. Then she would get up and wash and dry the breakfast dishes and put them away. After that she made the beds and washed some clothes, cleaned the kitchen floor, and then sat and sewed and waited for her husband to get back from town.

One afternoon, about a week after Sarah confronted her husband, he arrived home from the village, and as he put the key in the door he heard groans coming from the parlor. He closed the door quickly behind him and cautiously moved to the sofa where he saw his wife writing in pain. Beads of sweat had broken out on her forehead and she seemed flushed and her breathing labored.

"What is the matter, Sarah?" he asked in a gentle voice. He moved closer to her and sat on the edge of the couch.

"Oh, Jeffrey," and she put her hands over her heart, "I'm not feeling well."

"Some peppermint tea might help, yes, Sarah."

"Yes, perhaps, yes." and her groans became louder.

The Reverend rushed to the kitchen and opened cupboards and boxes and tins to find the peppermint leaves. Then he poured boiling water in a cup, added honey and brought it to his wife. She sipped the tea in between groans, and when she had half- finished it, she gave her hands to her husband. He held them gently and noticed how hot and sweaty they felt.

"Sarah, would you like me to get Doctor George?"

"No, No. Read to me Jeffrey. Read from the Bible. I need the Lord's forgiveness."

"Forgiveness, why Sarah, what have you done?"

"I did not mourn my sister, and she knows it. Oh, God, I tried to do good, but I failed. A good word from my sister now would do me good, do me better good than all of the medicines in the world."

"Sh, Sh, but why should your guilt make you feel so ill, Sarah. Tell me the truth now. What have you done?"

"I, I did not mourn my sister. I should have mourned her death. Now mine is coming and the guilt is too much."

"Sarah, what do you mean? Speak to me."

But only silence came. The Reverend looked at his wife, writhing in pain and knew he had to get the doctor.

"I'll get the doctor, Sarah. You need a doctor."

"No, stay with me. Not now, stay with me. You can get the doctor later."

"We'll pray together then you must go to sleep."

The Reverend opened the Bible and read:

"… the heart of her husband doth safely trust in her so
He shall have no need to spoil…."

Proverbs: Chapter 31

"Do you really meant that Jeffrey?" she asked, cutting him off.

"Of course, Sarah, I always mean what I say." And he gazed at his wife with worry and concern, his brow knitting into creases and valleys.

"I wish I'd known that; now it's too late," Sarah said, interrupting his thoughts.

"What do you mean Sarah?"

"Night is coming, Jeffrey."

She became silent, a troubling kind of silence. The Reverend came closer and bent over her blanketed form and asked again:

"What do you mean, Sarah?"

"Remember our wedding, Jeffrey. It was oh, oh, so wonderful," and her tears fell freely this time. She did not try to hide her face, but lay there with tears rolling in rivers down her cheek.

"Remember? How could I forget, the church, the flowers, the sunshine, then the rain, mud, and difficulty getting back home," he told her.

She moaned again and answered, "This pain is too much; Dear Lord, forgive me."

"What have you done, Sarah? What is it, Sarah?" he asked, his voice becoming more urgent and suspicious.

"Because I'm here lying in bed, and that tells the world, I am a poor wife, a useless wife whose husband does not even want to look at her."

The Reverend suddenly turned his head to listen to a noise coming from the back door. The dogs were howling. He cocked his ears to listen again.

"Oh Dear God, Jeffrey, it's death coming to get me?" And she stretched out her hand to push him away. He kept looking at her, waiting for her to answer.

"What, Sarah, what did you do?" He lifted her hands from underneath the blanket, clasped them and looked directly into her eyes. "Tell me, Sarah, what have you done? " When she remained quiet, he said, "All right, I'll get Doctor George. But first, I'll take you upstairs to bed where you will be more comfortable. Reverend Jeffrey lifted his wife from the couch, cradled her in his arms and took her upstairs to bed.

After her husband left, the blankets felt heavy and tight. Her head throbbed and her eyes felt weak. Her breathing became more labored and she called out her husband's name. The dogs became quiet, and the only sounds were the sigh of the winds through the trees, and her labored breathing. The silence and the mournful winds outside her window troubled her. She opened her eyes a tiny slit, and when she looked she saw dark, swirling clouds in the bedroom hovering just above her eyelids. She called her husband's name again, and when no answer came she turned her head to face the blank wall again.

In the meantime, Doctor George and Reverend Jeffrey were having an urgent talk as the buggy galloped to the church house.

"I should have looked more closely when you took ill a few months ago, Reverend. I would probably have noticed something."

"But she seemed well, was eating and sleeping well, and never complained about much. But even her own sister, Mrs. Jeremiah, just before her death, seemed well and healthy too. Nothing seemed amiss then, and nothing seems amiss now," the Reverend explained.

When they reached the church house, they went straight upstairs to the sick room. They heard mumblings. At the door they listened and listened, but could not make out any of the words.

They entered the room and the doctor lifted the blankets and shook his head. He asked how long had she been mumbling so.

"Only just now, over the last hour." The Reverend answered. "It might be some kind of repentance."

"She's in a stupor, but is very much alive," the doctor said, listening to her fluttering heart. He opened his bag and took out a bottle of medicine, "to slow down her rapid heartbeat," he said, as he gave her a spoonful. And they bent down and put their ears close to her head to listen to her mutterings. They sat by her bedside, but could make out none of the words, except occasionally, "sister" and "Jeffrey" and "forgiveness."

The Reverend bent over his wife's form and asked her again what had she done that needed forgiveness. The doctor came close and they heard her say, "Yes, I did it. Dear God, forgive me."

"What did she do?" asked the doctor.

"I don't know. I think she may have harmed herself," the Reverend answered.

"Well, I find no proof." The doctor rested his hand on the shoulder of the Reverend and told him to be strong.

Her moans became faint, and more faint as the evening wore on. By six o'clock, the mutterings had ceased, and the house became as quiet as a graveyard. Evening shadows broke through the windows making all sorts of ghostly shapes on the walls. The doctor put his ear closer to her heart and listened again. No sound came. He lifted her hand and felt her pulse. No throb came. He put his stethoscope over her stomach, her arms, her heart. No sound came.

He threw an extra blanket to cover her, stood up, sat at the desk and wrote in his brown book: "Death By Unknown Cause."

He tried to speak to the Reverend, to tell him he must call the undertaker, but seeing the Reverend's dark, frightened face, he wrote his instructions in a note, left it on the desk, opened the door and left.

After the doctor left, the Reverend whispered to the evening, "No one will believe me, Oh God, another death in the house. No one will believe me." He lifted the blanket from her face. He looked at her, the stillness of the body that was alive only this morning. He stood for a long time, watching. The chill of the room felt like a morgue, and memories, good and bad came and washed over him.

12

Reverend Jeffrey ended his story. He looked around the room as though he had forgotten for a moment where he was. The grave faces of the Quaker family came into view. They were sitting in a semi-circle around him, their eyes riveted on him. They noticed his misty eyes and the elder Quaker stood up and came close to him. The Reverend put his hand over his heart, took several deep breaths, and said:

"My heart feels as though it has been racing uphill all day." The elder Quaker rested his hand gently on the Reverend's shoulder and kept it there until his heaving had quieted down. When his breathing had returned to normal, the Reverend stood up and said:

"So you see, I woke up one morning in the bosom of my church, and that same night I went to bed in Purgatory."

"And no idea how you got there," the elder Quaker said with much sympathy.

"No idea how I came to be in this situation, no idea at all," the Reverend answered.

"After Sarah's burial, I had to get away. I knew no one would believe anything I said. I didn't know how she died, and the doctor did not know then. The news of her autopsy was delivered the day I left Bellville. The newsboys were calling it out, "Arsenic in blood," "Arsenic in blood of

Reverend's wife," as I drove through town to get away. Who would have believed I didn't poison her?"

Then the Reverend paused. He remembered the arsenic was still lying somewhere in the house.

"Oh Dear God, the poison, I forgot to search for it and throw it out." And a fresh wave of regret washed over the Reverend. He clasped his hands and held them in the air.

"Now the poison is sitting where someone might find it?" one Quaker asked.

"Oh Dear God, yes; I forgot to search for it," and the Reverend's voice became a high-pitched wail.

"You are one of the persecuted, indeed. The cause of death sitting where they can find it. It is an unlucky turn of fate."

"Well, let's get you ready for your new life," one of the ladies said in a serene, quiet voice. "Don't go worrying about something that's not yet happened. You will have a new life here."

"Yes. No one, no one must connect you with the Reverend from Belleville," the elder Quaker pointed out.

As they spoke, rays of dawn came into the parlor and the grey house became more visible to the Reverend. He turned his head and noticed that they were gathered together in a large room, the room where he had spent the last few hours telling the story of his life. As he looked around the large room, a woman came to him with a dress, and scarf, and bonnet. She helped him pull the dress over his head and then tied the bonnet under his chin. Afterwards she put on the scarf over the bonnet to cover most of his manly face. They stepped back to look at his long flowing dress that covered his neck, and arms, and all the way down to his ankles. We have no ladies shoes that will fit, but those boots of yours are good enough for now, they told him.

"You must wear a dress while you are here. This will be the best disguise for you."

As they spoke, the sounds of sparrows twittering amongst the trees came through the open windows, and the yellow rays of the morning sun rising behind the barn poured into the room. "A beautiful day, indeed," the Reverend said. They nodded their heads in approval.

"I want to be of good use while I'm here," he said, turning away from the window to face the group of women with their solemn faces. Please put me to work, I can do anything, from butchering cattle to shearing sheep and more.

"There's work to be done, but not yet. Much commotion in town right now. Seems John Brown has been captured and set to be hung."

"John Brown! Oh what a pity. With my own trials, I've paid little attention to the news."

"The streets are full with newsmen and detectives, and soldiers and militia men to keep order, and thousands of people wanting to get a glimpse of John Brown," the elder Quaker told him. "When things quiet down, there is a parcel of runaways I want you to collect and bring here. And remember, you must wear female garb always, here and going out too. No one will be looking for a woman, so keep wearing your woman's clothing for as long as you are here," they warned him again and again. "Now onto some spinning and sewing."

The Reverend looked down at the female garb, and noticed for the first time the rustle the dress made as he walked with the women to the stock room to help them pick out wool for carding and spinning. As they gathered the wool, he looked out onto the expansive lawn, and the high iron gate he rode though the previous night came into view. He noticed, carved on the two gateposts, the words, " Peace, Equality, Truth." There was no need to ask his friends how or why it was put there. He knew the answer. He knew it. It made him feel good to be amongst these good people.

They spun wool late into the evening, stopping only to check on the apple dumplings simmering in heavy iron pots, and to shoo flies from the scrapples left to dry on the window sills. At dinner that evening, the Reverend helped two ladies carry food from the kitchen to the dinner table. Then he sat between the five children and the ladies. Afterwards, the elder Quaker blessed the food, and blessed everyone at the table. The Reverend took his queue from the elder Quaker. They ate the simple meal slowly, almost as though it were a mere sense of duty, with no enjoyment or outward satisfaction showing on their faces. They ate in silence. At the end of the meal, they closed their knives and forks by laying them intertwined together on their plates. Then they snuffed out the candles. That signaled the end-of-meal-prayer will begin. The Reverend rose and blessed the end of the meal.

And every night and every morning, the Reverend got down on his knees and asked the Lord to keep the household safe. And every night and every morning as he prayed, he heard the runaway slaves hidden in the attics, and in the barns gathering together to begin singing their morning and evening hymns, hymns that carried him back to a time when he was little boy on a plantation in South Carolina. During those moments, dark memories washed over him and he remembered the worn faces of slaves coming home from the cotton fields at dusk, their mournful singing that went on all evening and late into the night until every last one had gone to bed.

One morning, a week after the Reverend came to the grey house, the Quaker family rose early as usual, said their morning prayer, and then told him he would be going to town today. The Reverend dressed in his usual female garb, but this time he wore a black veil to cover his entire face. When he was fully dressed with the veil and hat covering his manly face, he mounted a covered buggy filled with vegetables and fruits to take to market in Longsmills.

"Take the old Indian trail for ten miles," the elder Quaker told him. "You will know the trail by two wooden columns about twelve feet apart, about three miles down the turnpike. Go through that trail for about ten miles, and unload the buggy to a Mr. Beckwith. Afterwards, you will hear a hoot call. Follow that sound. It will lead you to a parcel of runaways. Bring them back with you."

"What if someone stops the buggy and ask about the runaways?" the Reverend asked.

"No need to worry. The runaways will be covered up with blankets and well-hidden deep inside the buggy. No one will stop a Quaker and ask to search a buggy, because we are always driving to and from the markets with fruits and vegetables and various household goods."

Feeling satisfied that he would be safe from wandering eyes, the Reverend whipped the buggy and rode to the marketplace. Along the old Indian trail, he passed old buffalo hides and bones, remnants of brightly colored wool blankets, brightly painted totems, all left behind by families of Native Indians on the move. Nearing town, stately oaks and weeping willows rose up and shaded the path. He felt at ease; his heart felt calm and sober. He had met no one and he finally felt safe. He was doing good work, the kind that always made him go back to a happier time in his life, when he was a young boy waiting to grow up. Back to a time when every morning that he looked up at the blue sky, he felt the sunlight flowing through him from head to toes.

The Reverend arrived at the crowded, noisy marketplace with wagons, carriages and buggies vying for space, and peddlers calling out their goods for sale. Amidst the hustle and bustle of the place, he spotted a poster on a wall announcing a reward of $500.00 for the capture of a fugitive. His heart gave a sharp thud and his body became limp. He moved slowly through the crowd to look closer. There on the wall he came face to face with a sketch of himself. He stared at the poster, his pounding heart threatening to jump out of his chest. He looked away, then looked again, then casually moved straight ahead, stopping once to ask for Mr. Beckwith. He found him and unloaded the buggy, all the while listening for a hoot call.

Above the din of the marketplace, he heard the hoot call. "Hoot, Hoot, Hoot," came the bird call. He turned to face the direction of the call and followed it until it led him away from the building. Ahead, sitting underneath a live oak, he saw someone in a buggy whistling a hoot call every few seconds. He followed. The driver was dressed in Quaker garb and inside covered up underneath blankets was a group of five adults and six children. The runaways got out, mounted his buggy without a word, and curled up deep inside underneath bags and parcels and blankets. As the Reverend rode back to the grey house, he heard the runaways softly humming and praying a long chorus of "Glory Be's," and "Hallelujahs," to God for leading them out of the wilderness.

When the buggy turned into the iron-gate, he heard the group stirring and their praying getting quieter. It was as if they knew they were near the house of mercy. He wondered how they knew. The buggy stopped, and one by one they jumped down and stood facing their new home.

"Good, good service, Reverend. Now we must find them a hiding place," the elder Quaker said.

The Reverend did not reply, instead he took the elder Quaker by the hand and led him to a corner of the barn, out of earshot of the group of runaways. He whispered, "I have to stay closer to home now, or go away from here."

"What do you mean?" How can you want to go away from here? You have done a mighty good job bringing these suffering people here," the Quaker asked passionately, taking the Reverend by the arm and sitting him down on an old bench.

"I saw my poster in the marketplace, with a $500.00 reward. It will only be a matter of time before someone caught on."

"A poster? Oh, a poster. If only that poster could talk, it would tell the whole truth. And what a story it would tell," the elder said, recalling the Reverend's story of a few days ago. "Well, we won't allow anyone to find you. No one must recognize you."

"You must stay here for now until after John Brown has been to the gallows. John Brown is still locked up in the courthouse, and he is to be taken to the jail to be hung. So things have quieted down for a while, but they will stir up again at the hanging. That was the reason today was a good day for you to go to town."

"Yes, Yes, I'll wait till then. I know I'm going to hate leaving this place." For two whole weeks afterwards, the Reverend remained in the confines of the grey house with its high walls and iron gate, the house that was always full of light from all the goodness that permeated its walls. He took frequent walks to the garden, pulled weeds from the cabbage and carrot beds, and helped to cut the wheat and corn. Now and then, he assisted in the shoemaker's shop, and the cabinet-making shop where he polished and rubbed leather and wood until they shone brightly. Each night he went straight to bed after the evening prayers, but found himself slowly tormented by the poster of himself in the marketplace. He began to wonder if any of the neighbors in the village suspected that the new Quaker living in the grey house was a fugitive from the law.

One night as torment raged in his head, and his mind drifted over the contours of his former life, an idea slowly dawned upon him. It descended like a mist out of the past, and as dawn broke, the shape of his idea was clear, and it stood boldly in front of him. He would travel to town. He had a tremendous urge to see John Brown, to be a witness to what will become of this abolitionist. With so many people moving about to witness the hanging of John Brown, he too would move about and join in the throng going to and from the jailhouse. He would disappear into the crowd and no one would give him a second look. In that way, he would be sparing the good Quaker family from any unnecessary scrutiny.

That morning after prayers, the Reverend stood up from the breakfast table, dipped his hands in his pockets and brought out a handful of silver coins. He placed them on the table, and pointed to them.

"These are all I have to give you; your love and mercy deserve more. But in case I do not return to this house again, please take these as a token of my devotion to you."

"In case you don't return? Why, where are you going?" asked one of the women, concern written plainly on her face.

"I'm going to town; perhaps I'll be lucky to get a glimpse of John Brown. Something tells me I should go. I don't know why," he stuttered, trying to find the right words. "I have a need to see John Brown before it's too late. I might even get lost in the crowd and no one will notice me."

"Perhaps, perhaps, but you are still taking a risk leaving this house." After a short pause, the elder Quaker continued. "But if you must go, May God go with you, and may His grace keep you safe." One by one, the family members came and shook hands with the Reverend, their faces grave and dignified. It was as though they knew it would be a long parting.

"Here, take this map with you. We don't have much to give you, but this will show you the way," the elder Quaker said. It is a map of all of the houses of mercy, between here and Canada.

They will receive you should you run into any trouble. Take it with you to wherever the road may lead."

The Reverend took the map and unfolded it.

"Yes, this will show me the way all right, a lost wandering soul in this cruel world."

"This, and God's love we give you. May God Bless you."

"This is more than I could ask for. Thank you!"

"We'll send a driver with you. He'll bring back a parcel of runaways. I hope you'll return to us when you can," and the two shook hands again.

"And, do not speak to anyone, unless you must." One of the women reminded him quickly. "You don't want your man's voice to give you away."

The Reverend nodded, smiled and pulled a black Quaker dress they handed him over his head. He tied the black veiled bonnet over his head and face, ran his hands over the dress to smooth it down, then moved around the room and took the hand of each member of the family and held it to his lips. No other word passed between them; none was necessary. He headed to the front door, and mounted the buggy. The driver whipped the horses and they drove through the high iron gate and headed down the road. The Reverend looked back twice, marking the image in his mind, as though he knew he would never see the grey house again, the good, simple house of mercy that had received and rescued him.

•

13

In town, the Reverend got down from the buggy, and pushed his way through the tightly-knit groups of people on the streets of Charlestown. He stood still and took in the sights and sounds, the excited faces moving aimlessly along, and the rows of well-dressed velvet-lined buggies and carriages. He heard loud voices and excited whispers, the hurried hoofs of horses galloping through the crowd, and the crowd making way for them. He spotted lines of soldiers marching up and down Main Street.

Up ahead, the Reverend spied a crowd following behind a line of militia men surrounding what looked to be a horse-drawn cart. When the Reverend came closer, he saw John Brown strapped to his own coffin, being carried in a cart through the streets of Charlestown from the courthouse to the gallows. When the cart passed in front of the Reverend, he looked John Brown directly in his eyes. He remembered the stories that said few men are able to look John Brown directly in the eyes, so mesmerizing were those eyes. Reverend Jeffrey looked into those eyes again, and again. Runaway slaves and freed negro women with babies and young children held them up so John Brown could kiss them. Others, seeing him tied down to his own coffin turned away, terrified at the image in front of them. Then the Reverend heard scornful voices jeering out.

"Onwards to the gallows, John Brown."

'Judgement day, John Brown."

Confusion and noises and voices vied with each other until he heard a voice blaring from a bull horn, "Attention. Attention. Everyone, your attention, please. Please go home. The streets of this city are not safe. Go home. Anyone caught on the streets after 6p.m. will be questioned. Please go home."

The Reverend stopped to listen. The crowd around him did not scatter. Instead they stepped forward following the coffin of John Brown as if they were being carried effortlessly by a wave of determination. Reverend Jeffrey looked up at the village clock - 4p.m. He followed behind them, moving along by the will of something. They reached the prison gates and the crowd came to a full stop. They looked on while John Brown and his coffin were pulled from the cart and lifted onto the shoulders of four men and carried into the jail. The crowd stood looking to the heavy wooden door through which John Brown entered, as though waiting to see him re-emerge. They stood by the prison gates for a full hour. Only when daylight began to fade did they start to thin out, but Reverend Jeffrey did not leave. He stood and said a silent prayer. Then he moved away from the gates, turning around every now and then to peer into the dark, as if to imprint the scene in his memory.

Reverend Jeffrey continued to walk the streets inhaling the sights and sounds. He noticed that some people, perhaps seeing him for the first time, stared at the strange woman dressed in black from head to toes, with a veil tightly drawn against her face. He became anxious. Some shook their heads in pity and whispered about the strange woman.

"Poor thing," the Revered heard. "She must be in mourning. Seems walking without aim. Gone clean out of her head, I 'spect. Can see every last sense gone, I'm sure."

"Yes, just like the old widows who wall off themselves in black for years and years and then lose all their senses."

His anxiety ceased and The Reverend smiled behind his veil, because it seemed to them, he was in mourning and has lost all of his senses, and he was glad.

As Reverend Jeffrey walked about, he noticed a few solders and news-men, some with pencils, scribbling furiously in their notebooks. He turned the corner to avoid them. As he came around the corner, he heard a voice that seemed to be addressing him.

"Ma'am, not safe to be out on a day like this, would you like a ride somewhere?"

The Reverend shook his head several times, but did not turn around and did not speak. He moved away and found a spot underneath a live oak across the street from a small park in the center of town. Before long, two reporters, their heads glued to their notebooks, came alongside the street and stood underneath the live oak tree. Half-an-hour passed and the sol-diers and reporters moved up and down the streets, but the Reverend kept moving to the other side of the square to avoid them.

When he had found a safe spot at last, he stood still and allowed a strange new feeling to wash over him. It was a feeling of fear tinged with a sense of freedom. With this new sensation, he allowed himself to think about his awful predicament. For the first time in many weeks he found some time to think about his calamity, and his mind drifted back to the little church house, to the place where his life began to unravel. He won-dered what little or big thing he had missed that might have saved him from his present predicament.

As he stood there, sensations of all kinds flowed over his being. He thought of those joyous years of his youth when his heart would bubble up with happiness each morning that he opened his eyes to God's blue skies above, when he knew his one and only reason for living was to become a minister and spread God's word. Those years were now gone, buried along-side his shattered dreams of saving ten thousand wayward souls, and his dream of preaching a sermon each and every Sunday morning until his eyes closed forever at a glorious old age.   Now he felt like a mere piece of the youth from so long ago. It was as though he had said good bye to a major part of himself, and all that remained was a skeleton of the person he once was.

For the first time since his predicament, a distinct thing came into his heart. It was not a sharp or even a dull thing, it was the feeling of being out of control, being unsteady, a feeling that said his life was headed to some sort of a cliff from which he would never be saved. It knocked out the sense of freedom he earlier felt. Regret and sorrow filled his heart.

He was glad he had run away from Bellville; had he stayed in the village, not even Heaven could have saved him. Not the Elders, not his good congregation, no one. He knew it as surely as he knew there was a God. The regrets stayed with him and he hung his head and allowed the tears to wash over him.

"Oh Good God," he called out.

Now, here he was in a place where no one knew him. Weeping lightened his heart and he lifted his veil and wiped the tears away.

As night began to close in around him, he knew it was time to go. It was past seven o'clock, but something, some unknown thing kept him riveted to Main Street. The bells of the village church rung out the seven o'clock hour, and the newsmen kept moving up and down the streets. They eyed the veiled woman who stood out amongst the thinned-out crowd, and they noticed she seemed distressed and agitated, and they wondered if she were suffering from some kind of illness.

"Can we help you, Ma'am," one reporter asked in a low, respectful voice. Are you a relative of John Brown?"

The Reverend answered with a shake of his head several times, the lacy veil fluttering in the evening breeze as he shook his head. He turned away from the two reporters, and stood at the other end of the park. But the reporters followed the veiled woman dressed in black. They had seen her before, yes, earlier that day. They watched and wondered silently about the strange woman as she moved away and started down the street. Their interest now peaked, they moved slowly down the road behind her. She turned her head to look back and seeing dark shadows moving towards her, she moved faster and faster down the road. The shadows moved faster, keeping several paces behind her, unable to tear their eyes away from the moving figure.

"Very unusual, very unusual indeed," one reporter pointed out.

"She may be unwell; let's keep her in sight." She's probably John Brown's relative. Perhaps she can tell us something about him, something that no one else knows. Let's follow her."

"You know, she might think we intend to harm her. She does not know we are newsmen."

"Perhaps, let's slow down, no need to scare the poor woman."

"Perhaps, perhaps."

The Reverend, too frightened to look back again hurried down the road. At one point as he passed by a small milk shop, a hand reached out and grabbed him in and he disappeared into the dark.

"Come with me quickly," whispered the kind voice, "I'm still in town waiting for a parcel of runaways to come in."
"Oh, Oh, Jonah, is that you?"

"Yes, yes, the one and only. Walk a few steps to the right, over here," Jonah ordered.

"Thank you Jonah, Praise be. How did you find this place?"

"It is my own, a place where I sell milk in the early mornings, and then I work at the Quaker house for the rest of the day. Reverend, I've been following and watching you to be sure no harm comes to you."

"I'm thankful, and so glad to see you here in the dark Jonah. God sent you, so thankful for His mercies."

"Shh, shh, we will sit here in the dark and wait. They are still out there," Jonah warned.

They sat quietly in the dark, listening to buggies and horses rambling up the street and down the streets. Sometimes footsteps came close to the shop then died away. Sometimes whispers came clear and loud, sometimes fearfully urgent, other times quiet and resigned. Someone asked, where did the veiled woman disappear to. She is ill; we must find her, the two in the shop heard the voice say.

Towards morning, when the night noises had finally died down, Jonah slowly opened the door and peeked out to the early morning sounds. He saw the butcher in his white apron pushing a wheel barrow full of grunting pigs to the market, a few farmers in the hay wagons driving a steer or two to the market, a few street sweepers with brooms and brushes. The reporters from the night before were nowhere around.

Jonah opened the door of their hiding place a bit wider and the sounds of the blooming morning came right in.

"I'll take you to the nearest railroad station. Remember, do not speak to anyone. I'll go in and get your ticket."

"To anywhere," the Reverend told him.

They hopped onto the buggy with the Reverend sitting in the shelter of the canopy and drove to the station.

Half-an-hour later the buggy arrived at the train station. The Reverend noticed a few people wandering about. Jonah hopped down and entered the ticket window. He whispered "New Hampshire" to the ticket master. A few seconds later, he handed the ticket to the Reverend. Holding her hand, he helped the Reverend down from the buggy. Jonah fussed with her veiled hat, straightening it and tying it tightly around the Reverend's neck. He picked off imaginary specks of dust from her dress. They waited by the buggy for the bell that called the passengers to board. They heard it and Jonah rested his arm firmly under her arm and led her to the doorway of the coach.

The Reverend stepped upon the first landing only to find his way blocked by two men. He looked up and found himself face to face with the newsmen of the night before.

"Hello, ma'am," one reporter said, and the fright bowled the Reverend off his feet. The Reverend tripped and the men held out their hands to steady him. "Please tell us why you ran away last night? We were only trying to help you." You seemed in distress. Our conscience told us to find you, to make sure you are ok. So here we are and we are glad to see you are ok."

The Reverend raised up his voice a few octaves before saying, "Why were you chasing me? Can't a woman walk alone on the streets without being harassed?"

"Madam, we were not chasing you. We merely wanted to know if you were in some sort of danger; you seemed to be suffering so. Are you a relative of John Brown?"

At that moment, Jonah called out to the Reverend.

"Mistress, is something the matter. Are these men bothering you?"

"They say they want to ask a question," he answered in his high octave.

Turning to Jonah, one reporter asked. "Did you say, mistress? Is this person your mistress?"

"Gentlemen, my mistress is in mourning. Come ma'am, let me take you home."

"Then why do you allow your mistress to wander the streets alone at night?"

"I wanted to be left alone to mourn, so Jonah did just that; he left me alone."

"Ma'am, I can tell you are in difficulty," one reporter said, ignoring the Reverend's reasoning. "Perhaps if we can't help, someone else can, maybe a doctor, or a minister of the church might better be able to get you the help you need."

"No. No. No. I need no one; I'll manage just fine."

"Please gentlemen, my mistress must come with me," Jonah cut in.

Ignoring Jonah, the newsman continued, "Madam, my conscience won't let me leave you here alone with your servant. He has allowed you to walk the streets alone. You will not go with him; you must come with us."

The newsman tried to take the Reverend's hand, but he snatched it away. The two reporters moved closer to her, surrounded her and they tried to lift her into their buggy. She wrestled with them, kicking and pulling and shoving them away. Suddenly, they bodily picked her up and pushed her half-way into the buggy, but she jumped out and her dress was caught on the spokes of a wheel. The men reached out to catch her from falling, but grabbed her veil instead. Bonnet and veil fell from her face revealing a manly, bearded face.

The newsmen looked at him in confusion. "Oh, who are you, mister?"

"No one, just a body in mourning," the Reverend replied humbly, amidst the outrage and indignation boiling in his heart.

"Mister, when a man dresses up as a woman, it looks doggone suspicious," one reporter admonished him.

"There's nothing suspicious at all. I'm merely in mourning, and I will be all right in a few days."

"Well, mister, it seems to me that your sorrows have broken your senses. You are acting strange, strange, indeed."

"Perhaps, perhaps," the Reverend tried to appease them. "Now, will you please let me be?"

"Please. Let me carry her home," Jonah pleaded again.

"Mister, come with us. We'll get you the help you need."

"Help will come only from the One above," the Reverend tried to tell them.

"No, we will take you to a hospital, only fifteen minutes away. Come with us," and they held out their hands to help her into the buggy. This time, the Reverend held out his hand and they made space for him in the buggy. They rode quietly through town. Behind the reporters' buggy, Jonah quietly rode his, waiting for the moment when the Reverend would need him. As they neared the hospital in town, one newsman noticed an excited knot of people gathered around a poster nailed to an oak tree. The buggy crawled to a stop and one of the reporters jumped down to take a closer look. He pushed his way through the crowd and came face to face with a drawing of the Reverend, the man in his buggy. The reporter ripped the poster from the tree and returned to the buggy. He showed it to the Reverend.

"What say you sir, are you a wanted man?"

"No, no. I've committed no crime, but I'm a wanted man," the Reverend said humbly, pulling the veil onto his face again as though to hide his shame.

"God help you mister, what do you mean?"

"Dear God, help me," the Reverend called out in distress. "I did nothing wrong."

"Then we must take you back to Bellville, according to this poster. They will decide there if you are a wanted man or not."

By now, a large crowd had gathered to witness the exchange between the reporters and the person with the bearded face from the poster. The Reverend tried to jump from the buggy, but the crowd surrounding the buggy stopped him. The newsmen pulled on the reins and the buggy galloped through the crowd. At the moment that the horses began to gallop away, the Reverend felt a nerve-shattering impulse come over him. The impulse told him to jump; jump, it kept saying. He cast his eyes towards the two reporters who wanted to help him, and he looked up at the bright sunny morning shimmering through the leaves, and the birds tooting their song. Nature was wonderful and God was speaking to him. He decided he would not jump. He looked back and saw Jonah still riding slowly, cautiously behind them. "The Good Lord in Heaven knows all things we mortals can never see," he whispered. The galloping horses sped up and drowned out any sounds for miles around. He looked back again; Jonah was out of sight, left behind by the speeding buggy.

14

That same evening, a telegraphed message made its rounds in Bellville. It announced that Reverend Jeffrey would arrive in town by train the next morning, in the company of newsmen. Mr. Phillip, the storekeeper and post master received the news and sent it to the Elders, the Women's Suffrage Guild, the Temperance Society, and other important organizations in town.

So Belleville lay asleep in the wee hours that morning until the church bell rang out the four o'clock hour. Then the town came to life. Mothers woke up small children and dressed them in Sunday shoes. Older children, glad to get a day off from school, wiped the sleep from their eyes and hurried down the land to town. Belleville stepped out in the cool morning to see their minister back in town. For half-a-mile on the road leading to town, people lined both sides of Main Street. Patrolmen with night sticks walked the streets. When Reverend Jeffrey's coach pulled into town, a large crowd of villagers and worshippers from the Olivetti Church was there to meet him. Some jeered, some wept, others stood in awe of the man they once looked up to.

"Reverend, what say you sir, did you do it?' someone in the crowd called out.

"We know you didn't, Reverend," others called out.

"God bless you Reverend. A thousand shame on the one who did it."

"Reverend, if you did in that poor woman, then may God help you."

The train slowed down in front of the courthouse prison. Three men, dressed in blue uniforms with badges and carrying night sticks, approached the coach as it pulled in.

"Is this our prisoner, one Reverend Jeffrey Masters of the Olivetti Church, Bellville?" asked one of the three detectives.

The Reverend heard them call his name. He bowed his head, unable to believe the calamity that his life had become. Great beads of sweat broke out onto his face and neck in the cool December morning. He felt rough arms grab him, pull him from the buggy and push him forward. He looked around and saw that he was in the midst of three detectives and four soldiers who were leading him into the courthouse prison.

They stepped briskly through a long covered pathway to the prison, a two-story building attached to the rear of the courthouse. For several minutes he heard the footsteps of doom moving him forward. They mounted two flights of steps and entered the front door of the prison. Three soldiers lifted the heavy wooden door covered with heavy iron spikes off its hinges and pushed it open. They walked down a long dark passage, stopped at a locked cell surrounded by wooden partitions, and waited. The Reverend felt like a small child waiting to hear his fate. He lifted his hands in silent prayer, until he was interrupted by the heavy boots of someone coming down the dark passage way. The Reverend turned his head and his eyes met shiny polished boots coming towards him. It must be the jailer, he thought. The pair of boots stopped in front of the locked cell and the jailer whipped out a ring full of dozens of keys, flipped out one about 16 inches long and unlocked the door. When the door opened, the Reverend winced. He was roughly pushed inside and the sound of the door locking behind him was like being locked alive in Hell. For a while he could not breathe, then slowly he looked around the little cell and noticed a barred window. It gave him breathing room and he heaved a small sigh of relief.

After a few hours of restless sleep, the Reverend got up out of bed and peered through the bars of his little window. There was a full moon. He kept watch, using the moon to tell the time. From experience, he knew that when the moon rested over the church steeple, it was about 3:00 a.m. I must stay awake through this dreadful night, he whispered to no one. I will not close my eyes. But when the early morning noises of the town stirring to life came into his cell, his eyelids felt heavy and sleepy, and he went back to bed.

Still restless and anxious, the Reverend opened his eyes an hour later to the sounds of voices outside his window. He got up and sat on the edge of the bed and listened. Out of the corner of his eyes, he saw several pieces of paper, folded neatly, fluttering through the bars of his window and onto his bed. He picked up a few and opened them. They were little notes written by various people: some telling him not to despair; some saying that God had his eyes down there in the cell with him; others, that they wanted him to get out soon, so they could hold up their sick babies and children for a kiss and a blessing. The Reverend was moved. He felt a calm come to his heart, as though God Himself had written those notes to give him strength and sustenance. At that moment, he got down on his knees and said a special prayer for the sick and the dying and the dead amongst the villagers of Bellville.

With the Reverend down on his knees several times a day, the rest of the week passed peacefully for him. At the end of first week, the trial of Reverend Jeffrey began. Accused of premeditated murder of his wife, the Defense would argue that The Reverend had not committed murder. Instead, his unloved wife had killed herself out of desperation.

The streets around the courthouse were lined with carriages, and buggies and horses and mules. A festive crowd from near and far, some with children and babies in carriages, some with picnic baskets and liquor, gathered outside the courthouse. People hung from tree limbs and roof tops to get a glimpse of the Reverend being taken from his jail cell to the courthouse. When they spied him, his fettered arms and legs moving slowly towards the courthouse, solos and choruses rang out, "God's Salvation," and "hell's damnation," and assaulted the Reverend's ears.

The sweltering courtroom was packed. Stone-faced men sat tightly crammed onto benches on the main floor, and weeping women sat tightly packed in the gallery. Every now and then a shout or a scream, "he's in-nocent", or "only God knows," came from the gallery. The two groups, one sure of the Reverend's innocence, the other sure of his guilt, looked around the room at each other, like enemies sizing up the opponent. A large assortment of people kept coming into the courtroom. At one point, a wheelbarrow was pushed up to the entrance of the courthouse. A man without any legs emerged and crawled his way into the room and sat on the floor in the back.

Not far from the Judge's desk stood a table, covered with white cloth on top of which sat several vials and test tubes. Inside of each tube there seemed to be various amounts of a white substance. On a second table sat glass bottles of various sizes. These were labeled with the dead woman's stomach, liver, spleen, intestines, bladder and kidneys. Those in the court-room heard shouts and screams from outside the building. They turned their heads to listen.

At that moment, the Reverend with four guards entered the court-room. His feet were still fettered, but his arms and hands were left free to touch the Bible and to swear the Oath. A deafening hush filled the room as the Reverend entered and sat at the Defense table. The Judge, dressed in all black morning suit, with red velvet collar came out of his chamber and those in the room stood and turned to face him. He stepped towards a high table and sat down, and with his quilled pen, he scribbled something on a document sitting on his desk. Reverend Jeffrey, without seeing it, knew the judge had just recorded the day and time, and the sunny weather pouring through the windows.

Reverend Jeffrey cast his face down and focused on the floor in front of him. For several minutes he seemed lost in his own despair, neither hearing nor seeing the goings on in the courtroom. Then suddenly he heard the Prosecutor's loud bass cutting into his thoughts. Reverend Jeffrey looked up to see a stout, bald-headed man with a lively paunch, and a pair of wide-rimmed glasses hung around his neck pointing to the table full of test tubes.

"Yes," said the Prosecutor, "those vials sitting over there contain the entrails of the dead woman. Each vial contains several milligrams of a white substance called arsenic, taken from the dead woman's organs."

There was a loud gasp and several moans as the packed courtroom listened to the gory details. Some covered their faces, some covered their ears to avoid hearing and seeing. Then they heard the Prosecutor call Reverend Jeffrey to the stand. The room became silent and the Prosecutor waited while the Reverend took the Oath. Then he continued:

"Reverend Jeffrey, please tell the courtroom how the white substance came to be in your wife's stomach?"

"She took it. She told me so. She took it," Reverend Jeffrey quickly answered, as though the words were begging to be spoken and came spilling easily off his tongue.

"Where and when did your wife give you this piece of information?"

"On her death bed. I told her I would send for the doctor and the minister, and that was when she told me so. She told me so," he answered, his voice quick and flustered.

"For the minister? Why send for the minister? Are you not a minister, Reverend Jeffrey?"

Reverend Jeffrey stared up in confusion at the indignant face bearing down on him.

"Well, yes, I, Yes, I am a minister. And I wanted to send for a minister to give blessings. I knew I couldn't do it myself, my own wife, giving her final blessings. It was not something I ever felt I could ever do. It's not easy to give someone final blessings."

"Did you send for the doctor?"

"Yes, yes. Of course I did."

"One more question, Reverend. Do you know why your wife may have taken the poison?"

The Reverend shook his head several times as if to ward off a slap that had just landed on his face.

"She had always accused me of not loving her. So perhaps that was her reason."

"Reverend, are we to believe that your wife took poison because you did not love her?"

"Yes, that was her reason," the Reverend said, his voice now firm and defiant.

"Was that her reason, Reverend, or is it *your* reason, Reverend?"

"What do you mean?"

"Reverend, there have been various rumors circulating about your heritage, about who your real parents are."

The question was sudden and it stung. Reverend Jeffrey's eyes widened in fright as though something had suddenly cut off his breath. He took a gulp of air before answering.

"My heritage? What does this have to do with anything?"

The Defense leapt out of his chair and called objection," What does this have to do with the case at hand?"

The Prosecutor tuned to the judge. "Everything, your honor; it will show the court how truthful this Reverend really is. Reverend, please tell us who your real mother and father are," the Prosecutor continued without waiting for the judge to respond.

"Who, or what my heritage is does not matter to God, and it should not matter to man." The Reverend said firmly. "It should not matter, but that I am a God-fearing man, I speak the truth, I do onto my fellow man as I would onto myself, and I follow God's Ten Commandments. What else can I say?"

"Please tell us who your parents are, good Reverend," the Prosecutor continued patiently.

There was silence as the room waited for the Reverend to speak. Feet shuffled and bodies squirmed in their seats. The Reverend, looking hard at a spot of grease on the floor in front of him, did not reply. Agitation began to swell up into his heart, and little veins popping up in his temple began to throb. He lifted his hand and rubbed them slowly all the time wondering what had become of his mother.

"My parents. Who my mother was or is should not matter to anyone. That she was a slave woman does not matter to God. Why should it matter to you or anyone else?"

Gasps and sighs filled the room.

"So, Reverend, your parishioners, the very people you administer to, the people you tell each and every Sunday to tell the truth, those people have no idea who you really are?"

"They most certainly know who I am. You, on the other hand do not know who I really am."

"So, good Reverend, you've been living a lie your entire life. Why should we believe you are now telling the truth - that you did not murder your wife with poison when we know you are capable of lying?" the Prosecutor pointed out.

"Lying, lying did you say? No, I am not lying. I am a human being who was raised to serve God. That is who I am. I was born out of grief and violence, yet, raised to serve the God who stirs the human heart to do good."

"Thank you, Reverend, thank you."

By now the Prosecutor had tightened his jaws and his shoulders had become rigid. He knew he had lost some face with the Reverend. He could tell that the Reverend's congregation and some of the villagers of Belleville had been stirred in a positive way by the Reverend's answers. He wondered if the jury had been so moved. So the prosecutor stepped up to the jury box, rubbed his hands together, as if they were on fire, leaned forward and unleashed his last poisoned dart.

"The last fact I'd like to point out to you, gentlemen, is this: The autopsy shows that Sarah, the Reverend's wife was a virgin when she died."

Horrified gasps and wails filled the courtroom. Three women from the gallery bellowed out like creatures in distress, and ran weeping from the room. Chairs and tables toppled over. Some fainted and had to be taken away on stretchers from the room. The judge called for order, but it took a good three minutes for order to be restored. Then the Prosecutor, seeing the effect of his well-aimed dart, smiled and continued.

"A virgin, gentlemen. Yes. Imagine, a married woman of four months still being a virgin," and his voice was profound and condescending.

The Prosecutor then turned to face the Reverend again. "Reverend, would you please tell the court why your wife of four months was still a virgin?"

The chaos was beginning to mount again, and the judge called for an hour's recess.

In that hour, the Reverend sat on the bench beside his defense lawyer. He rested his head on his arm and his mind wandered away to the little house in Bellville where he had lived for almost one year, the humble church house where he hid runaways slaves, and where he wrote some of the best sermons ever put before any congregation. He thought of all the people he had helped in small ways and big ways. Yes, he was glad he had helped them when he could. He thought of the corn and potato fields he worked, and the help he gave to pig and sheep farmers. He longed for those days when he would sit underneath a grand old oak tree after a long day in the fields, and listen to the earth breathe.

Then his mind drifted to his mother. The last glimpse he had of her was her figure walking away from the house on the day Mrs. Jeremiah sent her away. Regret filled his heart. He should have been sterner and had allowed her to stay. He was hers; the old slave woman, looking like a bundle of clothes moving down the road away from the house, was his. She was his and he was hers. He lifted his head. Noises from outside the courtroom brought him back to the present. He raised his eyes and looked out the window at the crowd gathered underneath trees and tents. Then he casts his eyes towards the sky. The sky seemed to him to be nothing but a blue grey haze, like a gauze hanging before his eyes. Nothing seemed clear anymore; nothing made sense anymore.

The hour ended with a blast of the midday horn from the roof of the courthouse. The Reverend was again called to the stand. He felt drained, a mental and physical wreck and could not answer the Prosecutor's question: "why was your wife of four months still a virgin?"

The Prosecutor stood still and waited for him to answer. Reverend Jeffrey shook his head several times. Then he turned to his defense lawyer, his eyes devoid of all hope.

The turn for the Defense came, and he moved up to the stand with defiant steps. The lawyer stood in front of the Reverend and gently rested his hand on his shoulder, and asked the Reverend if he had loved his wife. The Reverend looked into his eyes and saw compassion and mercy. It gave him strength, and he answered in a firm voice.

"I loved her as I do all of God's children."

"But as a wife?" the Defense coaxed him.

"As a wife, no. I needed time to see her as a wife, not just as one of my congregation. And to see myself as a husband. You see, she was forced onto me by her sister, and I needed time to feel what a husband should feel for his wife. So that was the reason she was still a virgin when she died."

"One more question, Reverend Jeffrey. Did your wife tell the doctor she had taken poison?"

"I think so, Oh, I, I, ..can't remember," the Reverend stuttered.

"That will be all, Reverend Jeffrey."

The Defense called Doctor Wilson to the stand. A dapper little man in coat tails wove his way from the back of the room. He walked with a limp, but a determined limp that said he was going to prove his knowledge to the courtroom to help the good Reverend.

"Doctor Wilson, please tell us what you saw when you arrived at the Reverend's house on the evening his wife died."

"The Reverend's wife was lying upstairs in bed. She was moaning and groaning in pain. When I felt her stomach, it was hard and rigid — not a good sign. I asked her what had she eaten that morning. She said, 'nothing.'

"And did she at any point tell you she had swallowed poison?"

"No. She said nothing about a poison, only that "she had done it."

"What do you mean doctor by, "she had done it?"

"I don't know, only 'that she had done it.' Those were her last words to me."

"Could you tell that her ailment was the result of eating poison, name-ly arsenic?"

"Yes, I suspected poison. Her eyes were dilated, her finger nails a deep blue, her skin had become darkish, and she was becoming unconscious right there before my eyes. She died without saying another word."

A roar went through the courthouse. Angry voices from the Reverend's church group came to his defense. The old legless man whom the Reverend used to visit and counsel, called out from his perch on the floor in the back of the room. His voice trembled with rage.

"Doctor, you said, eyes dilated, fingers blue? That's how my whole family died, of the small pox some years now," the legless man shouted.

"Silence, order." The Judge called out.

But the legless man continued, ignoring the one fact that arsenic was found in the stomach of the Reverend's wife. "My wife and three children died of the small pox, all in one week. So I should know. They all looked alike in death."

Silence filled the room as the villagers and church goers from Bellville listened to the last ray of hope from the no-legged man. The Reverend's fate was in the hands of the no-legged man and he was determined to de-liver for the Reverend and save him, the way the Reverend had saved him so many months ago. The judge kept calling for order, but the no-legged man repeated:

"All of my family died the same way. They all looked the same way in death: eyes dilated, fingers blue, skin black as night, just the way the Reverend's wife looked."

Hearing this, Reverend Jeffrey jumped out of his chair and grabbing his head with both hands, as though in pain, he tore through the roar.

"Oh, Dear God, I didn't do it. God knows, I didn't do it. I didn't hurt her."

"I believe him," a voice rang out. "Inside this heart of mine, I know the Reverend did not do it."

The Judge called for order again, but roaring, and shouting and weep-ing only became louder. Then another one stood up and raised his voice above the noise. "The Good Reverend straightened out me and my family.

Now I have a job taking care of my whole family. We don't care who his mother and father was. He proved himself ten times over already."

The Reverend became silent standing there. His eyes carried over to the group of his church defenders. He raised his hand and put it over his heart as a sign of thanks and blessing. Then he sat down and great drops of tears rolled down his cheeks. The courtroom burst into chaos again.

The Judge calling for order did not help. The weeping and shouting only became louder.

A few minutes later when the roar had lessened, the defense attorney continued to question the doctor.

"Doctor, for the benefit of the jury, please tell us the "cause of death?" What cause did you write on Sarah's death certificate?"

"I wrote 'Unknown.'"

"Why "unknown,' doctor?"

"At that point, I did not know for sure what the cause of death was - only an autopsy can tell."

"Thank you, Doctor, Thank You."

The Defense then called the senior Elder of Olivetti Church, Mr. Morrison. All eyes turned to the old man in the front row. He picked up his feet, leaned on his walking-stick and tottered up to the stand.

"Mr. Morrison, you have been a mentor to Reverend Jeffrey. Is this correct?"

"Yes, Yes, a mentor, a guide, and we three Elders intervene in matters public and private."

"Therefore, Mr. Morrison, you intervened, as you say, in the private lives of your parishioners."

"Yes, yes,"

"Mr. Morrison, did you intervene in the private life of Reverend Jeffrey and his wife?"

"Oh, yes, that we did, and would gladly do so again."

"Mr. Morrison, please tell us: Is the Reverend Jeffrey that you know, is that man capable of poisoning his wife?"

"That young man over there is no more capable of poisoning his wife than you or I."

"Tell us why you say that, Mr. Morrison."

"His wife was a vain woman who wanted to be first in his life. She told me so. Oh, that poor man should have been born a saint. In my eighty-something years on this earth, I've guided several young ministers to our church. He is the cream of them all in his will to do God's work first, last, and always. And that, my dear man, was too much for his vain wife."

"Thank you, Mr. Morrison. That is all."

A full minute passed in which the Prosecutor could not decide if he wanted to cross-examine Mr. Morrison or not. Then he stood up and turned to the jury box and made a short summation. He reminded the jury that Sarah died with arsenic in her stomach, and that she was a married virgin up to her last dying day. After he had made his summation, a series of hisses and hoots and frustrated groans came from the lower and upper levels of the courtroom.

When that had died down, the defense lawyer rose to make his point.

"Gentlemen of the jury, you are being asked to judge this man sitting here before you. Judge him only on what you have seen and heard here today. We know that his wife, Sarah, died of arsenic poisoning. Remember, no one saw the Reverend give his wife poison. The Reverend said she took it herself. Does that make sense? Is it possible his unloved wife took poison to kill herself? Ask yourselves that one question. Did his wife take the poison to kill herself. If your answer is 'yes, she took the poison herself,' then ask yourselves, why did she take it? If you can answer: because she felt unloved and ignored by her husband, then you must return a verdict of, "Not Guilty." Now it's up to you. Judge the Reverend on his own words, and on the facts of the case and only the facts. Thank You."

Shifting of bodies, and loud sighs greeted the end of the Defense's summation.

That afternoon, the jury left the room and began to deliberate the fate of Reverend Jeffrey. People stood outside and watched and waited. Some knelt where they stood and clasped their hands up to Heaven. Others sang their beloved hymns to keep their spirits from crumbling. Some wept, others whispered fearfully about the doom that awaited the good Reverend.

Three hours later, the horn on the roof the courthouse sounded the 5:00 p.m. hour. Chaos ran through the crowd again. Those on the outside waiting on top of buildings and underneath trees, rushed to get inside the courtroom to hear the verdict.

Inside the afternoon courtroom, there was standing room only. Heavily armed soldiers stood beside the Reverend as the verdict was read.

A guilty verdict rang out and touched the ceiling. It fell onto distressed women and stone-faced men who rushed out of the room as though it were on fire. The Reverend stood wide-eyed, unable to believe what he had just heard. He felt a powerful need to breathe. His lungs felt as though they were overflowing with water and there was no room to take a good deep breath. His head began to spin. He felt his heart jerking back and forth as though it were having trouble staying alive. He looked up and his eyes fell upon the crowd, their faces empty of hope. They were a lost mass rushing towards the exit. Just then he heard someone chanting, 'evil', 'evil,' 'house of evil.' Reverend Jeffrey felt more heavy chains fettering his hands, then his legs, and his body went limp and he fell to the floor. Just as he fell to the floor, the judge raised his hand, the room quieted and he passed judgment.

"Before I pass judgement on you, the convict, is there anything you would like to say, Reverend Jeffrey?"

But Reverend Jeffrey did not stir. The guards tried to rouse him, but he was still, fainted away into oblivion.

"What say you prisoner?" the judge repeated.

But the only sound was the loud, heavy labored breathing coming from the prisoner lying prostrated in the middle of the room. The judge looked around the room and seeing all the faces turned up to him, called for the Black Bible. He rested his hand on the Bible and read the words that would seal the Reverend's doom.

"Having been found guilty of the sin of murder in the first degree, it is the judgment of this court that you, Reverend Jeffrey Masters, be held in jail for a period of no more than one month, at the end of which time you will be hanged until you are dead."

Chaos broke out again, but the Reverend was still lying prone on the floor. After the judge passed judgement, the soldiers lifted him and carried him away to his cell.

When the Reverend woke, it was dark. He lifted his head from his cot and looked through the bars of his cell window to the outside. The whole world seemed normal. Glittering stars shone through the winter trees. The waning moon was in its descent, and the early morning noises, the horses clipity clopitying to the market and the shopkeepers pulling up their shutters, all came into the cell. Then he realized where he was. The prison cell, an alien thing that had no connection to his past or his present. He looked around the room again as if searching for something familiar, but all he saw was the dense darkness.

Reverend Jeffrey lay in bed feeling nothing, neither hope nor fear, only a tremendous numbness. He tried to remember what had happened in the courtroom after the guilty verdict. Nothing came to him, but he already knew what the sentence was: death by hanging. The numbness came even stronger than ever.

One hour later, even before it seemed the sunrise had hardly shown its rays, he heard what sounded like hammering coming from outside his window. He knew the sound, the rhythm of hammer hitting wood. As the sun rose higher in the sky, the hammering, sawing, and shouts, sometimes laughter, came into the prison cell and filled it up. The noises went on until late evening, picking up again next morning, and carrying on until evening. The Reverend knew what they were building, but he dared not look out the window. He did not want to see the thing that was waiting to seal his fate. After three days, his curiosity took over and the Reverend stood upon his bed and looked through the bars of his cell window, and there in front of him stood the half-completed gallows. As the gallows grew, so did his anxieties.

Each day, close to his cell, idle men and women drank whisky in the early morning, and cursed and fought each other in the evenings. Mothers hugged their children, and husbands and wives clung to each other for protection. The Reverend heard planters and slave owners discussing the price of cotton and tobacco, while they watched and waited and the gallows took shape.

One evening, the Reverend heard a chorus of voices singing outside his window. He joined in singing the well-loved hymn, "My Faith Looks Up to Thee, Thou Lamb of Calvary." His voice came softly at first then became louder and louder until it melded with those on the outside. He recognized the bass of Phillip, the shopkeeper, and the soprano of Mrs, Bailey. Their singing calmed his heart. For many days afterwards, the Reverend looked forward to the group coming to his window, lifting their voices high above the treetops, and comforting him. That night, for the first time since he stepped inside the prison cell, he knelt and prayed for deliverance from his sorrows. He was not afraid of death, he told the Lord; he merely wanted it to be peaceful. As he clasped his hands, he remembered the runaway slaves often telling him that death did not frighten them. Living frightened them. Living on a slave plantation, they said, was like living with one long disease that only death could cure. Their words comforted him now.

One morning, two weeks after the verdict, as he lay on his cot waiting for a sign from God, he heard voices outside his cell door. He looked up to see two men and a woman dressed in simple Quaker garb. It took Reverend Jeffrey a good minute before he realized they were his old friends from Virginia, his friends who lived in the grey house with the green trim, his friends who had protected and sheltered him when he needed it most. Reverend Jeffrey stood up and the guard opened the cell door and they entered. The Reverend smiled for the first time in four months. The three Quakers bowed but did not speak. The elder Quaker opened a Bible and the three sat on the Reverend's cot, and for a solid hour they hung their heads in silent prayer, except for occasional words of comfort from Deuteronomy, or from one of the Psalms that the Quaker read out loud, "…He will neither fail thee nor forsake thee; fear not, neither be dismayed." When the elder Quaker closed the Bible at the end of the hour and stood up, Reverend Jeffrey asked them to sit again.

"Thank you for reading from two of my favorite passages. But before you go, I want to tell you something, something you should know; it's about my heritage. I know it won't matter to you, but for the last two weeks I've been thinking I need to tell my story, for the sake of my old mother, the slave woman who raised me until age seven. The family, Hendersons, from New England bought me thereafter from my master in North Carolina. My story is no different from the hundreds who were sold, or who ran away from slavery only to end up in the North."

"I know my mother suffered greatly at losing me, perhaps crying bucketsful of tears at never seeing me again, and I suffered too at perhaps never seeing her again. But I thrived under my adopted family of two boys and two girls whom I now called sisters and brothers. When I turned twenty-one, my family sent me away to Bible school where I spent three years learning to become a minister. As I have said before, this was my calling; I've always felt so. My slave mother kept watch and seemed always to know how I was faring. When she heard I had become a minister, someone wrote to me on her behalf. She wanted to spend her last days with me. So she came to live with me at the church house. I am grateful to my adopted family, and to my slave mother for making me a God-fearing man. May God bless them and keep them in His mercies.

"Well done," the elder Quaker said. "May the Good Lord keep them in His mercy."

After the Quakers left, the cell suddenly felt chilly, like a morgue. Reverend Jeffrey called for a blanket and for the rest of the day, he wrapped himself in the blanket and lay on his cot until the voices outside his window woke him with their hymn of praise, " Oh Jesus I have Promised to Serve Thee to the End."

He joined in, his voice blending with theirs.

During the third week of his confinement he dreamed that his adopted family had come to see him. The vision seemed partly dream, partly real. When he opened his eyes next morning, there stood the six of them by his bedside, pain, love, and anguish written all over their faces. Before he could speak, he heard his father say. "We know you are innocent son; you are innocent, and you must save yourself."

"I have no courage father. What can I do to save myself? Nothing. I've been wondering, just the last few days, if there really is any salvation in this life. I know I am innocent, I've done everything right, have never done wrong to a single soul. Now here I am being treated like a criminal who has committed the ultimate sin. Where is the salvation that the Bible says should be mine?" he said, as though he had been waiting for a long time to tell someone of his thoughts.

"Don't say that, don't say that," his father whispered.

"I have no courage to save myself, none, I don't know how to save myself."

"You are a brave man," his father comforted him. "You are innocent, and yet you stand ready to die. You are very courageous."

"Every evening a group of dedicated villagers comes to my window to sing and to comfort me. They know I am innocent. And every single man, woman and child who knows I will die an innocent man showers me with peace and serenity to await that hour."

"Perhaps that is your fate, son. You will show others that there are things beyond our comprehension. God has sent those who believe in your innocence to comfort you."

"Yes, indeed they are a comfort to me."

"We feel better knowing you are not frightened or lonely as you wait to meet that hour," his mother said, running her hand through his hair.

There was little left for them to say to their son. They wanted to see how they could help him in the remaining days left, they told him, but instead, he has helped them lighten their own burden, the burden they would surely bear to the end of their lives, his father told him.

One evening, a few days before his walk to the gallows, a buggy pulled up near the prison gate. Several men jumped down and flipped the sheets off a wooden object. As they pulled it out of the buggy, frightened whispers moved through the crowd and reached the Reverend.

"A coffin, Oh God, 'tis the Reverend's coffin."

When the fearful whispers ran through the crowd still outside the prison gates, people stopped what they were doing and turned their heads and solemnly watched the four men life the wooden coffin and carry it into to the jailhouse. The Reverend looked out at the same time and watched the men lift the coffin onto their shoulders. The numbness returned.

His days now began the same and ended the same with no variations in between. Each hour seemed the same as the last one. When he went to bed at night, he no longer looked out onto the barred window. His head now turned to the wall, the blank stark wall where nothing interfered with his thoughts.

The night before his execution, the Reverend heard the group praying outside his window. They were reading the 23rd Psalm. As he listened he realized they were reading it backwards. He listened and listened. He remembered the old folks telling him that it was a sign of great love and respect to have the Psalms read backwards at any funeral. Reading it so was meant to keep the soul from wandering the earth in search of rest and peace. The Reverend clasped his hands towards Heaven. He felt at peace.

Next morning, a large unruly crowd gathered on roof tops, on tree-tops, on top of fences and upon ladders leaned against walls to witness the execution. As they watched and waited, the large wooden door of the jail flew open and Reverend Jeffrey appeared on the steps with a black hooded mask covering his head and face. His hands were tied behind him. On either side of the Reverend were the sheriff and the prison chaplain. The three walked slowly towards the gallows, past the horse and cart that would throw the pulley, their mournful footsteps filling up the morning air. The Reverend and the men mounted the ten wooden steps to the gallows and stood still as if waiting for a signal. The executioner, a man dressed in black suit and black hat, threw the noose around the Reverend's neck. Then he forced a white handkerchief in the Reverend's unwilling hand, the signal to the sheriff that he was ready. Several tense minutes passed while the executioner adjusted the noose and asked the Reverend if he was comfortable. Reverend Jeffrey's lips moved silently in prayer. The chaplain stepped onto the scaffold and gave him the last rites. A full minute passed when suddenly the white handkerchief fell to the ground.

There came the sound of a horn, and the horse and cart moved at a gallop. Amidst the sound of the gallop, gasps and cries, and jeers and cheers went out, and the condemned man began to swing from the scaffold. When the noises died down, those standing close to the condemned Reverend said they heard him heave a soft sigh, like a small distinct wave that came ashore, and then went back into nothingness, "never to crest no more."